HER WICKED STEPBROTHER

A NOLAN BASTARDS NOVELLA

AMY OLLE

Editing: Hot Tree Editing and Em Petrova
Cover Design: Michele Catalano Creative
Cover Photography: Wander Aguiar
Cover Model: Andrew Biernat

ISBN: 978-1-944180-10-2

To the insecure teenager in all of us

CHAPTER 1

"*M*arried?" An arrow of panic pierced Brynn Hathaway's heart. "But you just met."

A soft light came into her dad's eyes, the same light Brynn had noticed two weeks ago after he'd returned home from meeting his online girlfriend in person for the first time. "Sometimes when you meet someone, you just know."

Her fork, heaped with pasta salad, hovered midway to her mouth. "Know what?"

He reached for another piece of barbecue chicken. "That they're the one."

She frowned. "The one what?"

"The one you're meant to be with." At first, she didn't recognize the sound reverberating in her dad's throat, so rarely did he laugh. "Someday, you'll understand. Someday soon, I imagine."

Unsure what he meant, her scowl deepened. "Will I get to meet her soon?"

"She arrives next week."

"Arrives? Here?" Brynn squeaked. "Like, for good?"

His grim features softened. "Don't worry. You're going to love her. I promise."

But will she love me?

The sudden lump in her throat. "And the wedding? When will that be?"

"Soon. After they've had a chance to settle in."

"They?"

"Siobhan has three kids." His low, rusty laugh sounded again. "Three *boys*."

Brynn's fork clattered to her plate.

She'd always wanted a sibling. But three? Three boys?

Three *brothers*?

Brynn didn't know anything about brothers. Her best friend, Molly, had a brother, but Joey wasn't a good example of the typical male sibling. He barely spoke in complete sentences and spent all his time playing video games.

After dinner, Brynn raced upstairs and barricaded her bedroom door. She climbed onto the bed with her laptop and switched it on. Her fingers trembled as she stabbed at the keyboard and read about the home her soon-to-be family was leaving behind in Ireland and the flight that would deliver them to Chicago the following week.

In her ears, her heartbeat thrummed as she struggled to recall what her dad had said when she'd asked him the names of her new brothers. Something about his bride-to-be, Siobhan, naming each of her sons after a hero from Irish folklore. Brynn's hands flew over the computer keys.

Rory, the youngest of the three boys, had been named after a tenth-century Irish king while Cian, who was only a year older than Rory and about to turn sixteen, shared his name with a legendary warrior. Aiden, the eldest of the brothers, was seventeen years old, like Brynn, and derived his name either from the Celtic sun god and or a revered fifth-century Irish saint.

One last internet search revealed no heroes or gods, mythological or otherwise, shared her name. Instead, she learned that Brynn translated roughly to the Welsh word for hill.

A saint, a warrior, a king, and... a hill?

Tiny darts of panic jabbed, and she smacked the laptop shut.

In truth, the answers she most wanted couldn't be discovered by an internet search.

What would her new family be like? Would she like them? Would they like her, despite her unremarkable name? Would her new mom like her any better than her real mom had?

Everyone knew Brynn's mother didn't love her.

Her entire family knew it, including her aunt and uncle and all five of her cousins. The other families in their close-knit Chicago neighborhood knew it. And thanks to the cruel, loud-mouthed Samantha Whitaker, all the kids at school grasped the fact that Brynn's mom didn't love her only child enough to stay.

Most importantly, Brynn knew it.

Her mom's abandonment when Brynn was twelve years old had cratered a hole the size of Lake Michigan in her life. Not only had she lost her mom, but her even-tempered, affectionate father had fallen into a dark despair that, five years later, he'd never fully emerged from.

Another pang of fear had her snatching a notebook off the nightstand. Flipping it open, she scribbled a list of chores she needed to complete before their arrival.

Over the next week, whenever the panic rose up, she attacked another task on her list. She mowed the lawn and skimmed the leaves and insects out of the in-ground pool in the back yard. Indoors, stocked the kitchen cupboards with a variety of snacks and a host of ingredients, then she helped her dad convert the office upstairs into a bedroom that two of the boys could share. In the partially finished basement, they set up another space for the third boy to use as a makeshift bedroom.

She found the whole thing weird, buying food and picking out bedding for people she'd never even met.

The day before they would pick Siobhan and her sons up from the airport, Brynn cleaned every room in the house. She even scrubbed the bathrooms, making sure to close the doors after she'd finished so that her cat, Romeo, didn't turn on the faucets and leave a hairy mess in the sinks again.

The next morning, she cut a cluster of flowers in the garden and stuffed them into a clear glass vase. Their fragrant scent filled her nostrils when she set the vase in the center of the dining table and made a quick scan of the house.

Everything was perfect—as perfect as a home without a mother could be. For the first time since her dad had announced his intentions to remarry, a fragile bud of hope blossomed in Brynn's chest.

But while she waited with her dad at the airport baggage claim, her mind returned to her troubled thoughts. What should she say to the woman who would become her stepmom? What did she possibly have to talk about with teenage boys? She knew nothing about Ireland or video games.

When the first trickle of passengers flowed down the long corridor, a sheen of moisture kissed her skin. She glanced up at her dad, who searched the faces passing them by. Her mouth went dry and she licked her lips while she waited for the spark of recognition to alight on his features.

Bodies poured into the corridor, swarming like the butterflies in her stomach.

"Do you think she'll like me?" Brynn whispered.

But her dad had already shuffled forward. He lifted his arm and a strikingly beautiful woman with black hair strode toward them. With an unsteady smile, he raked his hand through his neatly combed light brown hair.

"Alan, my love." The woman stepped into his outstretched arms.

Under her breath, Brynn practiced the correct pronunciation of her stepmother's name—*Shiv-awn Shiv-awn Shiv-awn*.

The couple lingered inside their embrace, taking a moment to share a few softly spoken words while behind them, three strangers wearing three sullen scowls loomed.

Then suddenly Brynn found herself pinned by Siobhan's bright gaze. "You must be Brynn," she said, her smile as pretty as her lilting Irish accent.

Please love me. Please please please please.

Siobhan reached out, and Brynn drew close, until the cloud of sweet perfume enveloped her. She wanted to melt into the warm, motherly hug, but Siobhan withdrew her touch before Brynn had experienced its full impact.

"Boys." Siobhan gestured to the trio hanging back. "Come meet Brynn."

Every muscle in Brynn's body tightened as the three strangers fixed their dark gazes on her. "Boys" seemed an inaccurate term to describe them. Though lanky, they had wide shoulders, and the tallest of the three measured nearly a head above her dad.

"Hawareya?" The shadow of a smile touched the tall one's face. "Yer a wee one, an't ye?"

The skinniest boy snickered. "Dat's roy. Tow next to ya, we awll are."

Brynn's brain stumbled to keep up with their quick, melodic speech. Unsure what was being said, she looked to the third boy, who stared daggers at her from beneath the hood of his black sweatshirt.

Her heart thrashed against her breastbone harder and harder the longer he stared—glared—without speaking.

"Aiden, say hello to yer sister." Siobhan tugged the hood off his head.

Brynn gasped.

He had rich, dark hair and turbulent brown eyes that glittered with flecks of liquid gold. Sharp angles defined his cheekbones and jawline and the straight, elegant line of his nose. Only the callous sneer upset the perfection of his mouth.

"She's not me sister," he said, each heavily accented word spoken with cruel precision.

Despite the sting of his rejection, relief coursed through Brynn at that technical fact. He was not her brother, and thank the heavens for it. For one, if his dark scowl was any indication, he seemed more likely to murder her in her sleep than develop anything remotely resembling sibling affection. But more than that, what she felt when she gazed at his ruthlessly beautiful face could never in a million years be deemed sisterly.

A hot July sun mugged them when they exited the airport terminal and trekked across the heat-soaked parking lot to her dad's SUV.

While Siobhan claimed the front passenger seat, Rory climbed into the back with the mound of luggage, and Brynn somehow wound up wedged between Cian and Aiden on the middle row bench seat.

The length of her body pressed against Aiden's, and his heat seared her everywhere they touched. She snuck a glance at him and found her curious gaze immediately ensnared by his dark eyes. He held her captive a moment, then slowly turned his head to stare straight ahead.

Flushed and overheated, she inched closer to Cian, but as her dad steered the car through the airport parking lot and out into traffic, she became aware of the menacing grimace on his face. A shiver of alarm skittered up her spine.

Carefully, she tracked the target of his terrible scowl to the car's rearview mirror and her dad's reflection there. Reflexively, she shrank back, only to come up against Aiden's hard body once more.

She jolted. Shoving her hands in her lap, she kept her eyes facing the front of the vehicle as they barreled along the interstate.

Oblivious to Cian's death-glare, her dad chatted away, pointing out the soaring black monolith of Willis Tower and a few other landmarks visible from the car's interior. With a pang, Brynn observed the nervous waver in his voice.

At home, the stream of his chatter continued to flow as they hauled suitcases inside and dropped the hulking luggage in the middle of the living room. Though the open concept layout of the 1930s brick bungalow didn't necessitate a tour, her dad provided one anyway.

Brynn crept toward the stairs, trying to escape the chill from Aiden's ice-cold stare. But no matter where she sought to hide in the suddenly cramped living room, his dark gaze stalked her. Goosebumps prickled across her flesh and she rubbed a hand up and down her arm.

When her dad finally fell quiet, Siobhan laid a hand on his forearm. "It's a lovely home."

Brynn had never seen her dad blush before.

"Isn't it lovely, boys?" Siobhan faced her sons.

It must've been Rory who grunted.

Cian flopped onto the sofa and plopped his feet on the coffee table. "We had a lovely home in Ireland."

After that, everyone went in separate directions.

Brynn sought refuge in her bedroom, where she remained until night had fallen and the house had grown quiet.

Needing to brush her teeth, she padded barefoot down the hallway and opened the bathroom door—

She reared back at the sight of a naked male body. Wet from the shower, he'd flung a towel over his head and was rubbing his hair while steam and the fresh scent of body wash floated in the air.

Frozen, she stared, mouth ajar, at his smooth, taut skin. The temptation was too strong and her eyes fastened on his penis. She'd seen drawings of them in her health class textbook, but she'd never seen one in real life.

While she looked on, it started to grow—*and grow*—until the hard shaft stood erect against his flat abdomen.

Whoa.

The replica Ms. Norbury had used in class to demonstrate proper condom placement hadn't done the male member justice. Brynn's gaze roamed up his sleek, taut body. A shamrock tattoo stamped one of his hip bones, and his torso rippled with his movements. By the time she reached his face, he'd finished drying his hair and golden brown eyes watched her watching him.

A wicked smile played on Aiden's lips. "Like what ye see?"

She jumped as though scalded. "Oh my God. Uh... I... I... I...."

"It's all right. I can see ye do." He tossed the towel aside, seemingly unperturbed to be stark naked in her presence. "Do not tell me ma."

Shock had stolen her ability to speak.

He pointed at *it*. "She doesn't know about this yet."

The tattoo. He was talking about the tattoo. Why was he talking about his tattoo rather than covering his gloriously naked body?

Heat rushed to the surface of her skin, so hot she feared her body was on fire. Her soul seared.

She should leave. She knew she should leave. She should run as fast as she could from the magnificent sight of him, naked and wet and hard... *everywhere*. An audible gulp squeezed from her tight throat, but she didn't move. She couldn't drag her gaze away.

"If yer gonna stay, maybe ye wanna help me out here?" With an aching slowness, he smoothed a hand down his torso and gripped his rigid shaft.

She yelped and yanked the door shut. Whirling, she stumbled down the hall to her bedroom. Slamming the door shut behind her, she pressed her hands to her face.

She was burning hot.

For her freaking stepbrother.

CHAPTER 2

$\mathcal{B}$rynn couldn't stop thinking about *it*.
About him.

All of him.

She fell asleep with thoughts of him banging around inside her skull and woke to the clatter of him in her mind. She wanted to see more—to *know*—more about him. What did he like? What didn't he like? Other than her.

He obviously hated her, which shouldn't have surprised her. The kids at school kind of hated her, too. Most especially, Samantha Whitaker. But was there something, or someone, he didn't hate? She wanted desperately to learn the answer to that riddle.

The morning after their bathroom mishap, Brynn padded downstairs, her thoughts consumed with her older (by five months) stepbrother. Maybe, he didn't hate her as much as he hated being forced to leave his life behind and move to the other side of the world? She had to admit, had their situations been reversed and she'd just landed in a strange city in a foreign country, she'd probably have been a little grouchy.

When she reached the bottom stair, she spotted him at the

kitchen sink, drinking a glass of water and gazing out into the back yard. The air in her lungs seized.

He wore gray running pants, and his white T-shirt hugged his lean torso. A sliver of sunlight picked out the lighter strands of his dark hair, and the mix of russet and black fascinated her. Without her conscious consent, her gaze sought flesh, touching over the glimpse of skin at his collar and the muscles on his arms before winding up on his bare feet, which were lean and had a high arch.

What the hell was wrong with her that she found everything about him physically appealing, even his feet?

In her sleepshirt, she crept forward.

A nearly infinitesimal jerk passed through him when he detected her presence. His head whipped around and she found herself pinned beneath his stormy gaze.

"Hey," she said.

He studied her quietly for a moment, as though considering the most efficient, untraceable means to bring about her demise. Then, without a word, he set his glass in the sink and gave her his back as he turned toward the basement door.

When the sound of his footsteps on the stairs had faded, the breath returned to her body with a sharp kick. He'd truly mastered the hate-ignoring thing. Not even Samantha Whitaker could best him.

Later that evening, Brynn decided she wanted to cook dinner for everyone. If Cian or Rory, or even Siobhan for that matter, were disappointed or in any way upset by their sudden displacement, she wanted to give them something that might make them feel a little better.

Aiden, she wasn't worried about. He obviously had no feelings.

When it'd been only her and her dad, she'd often prepared small meals for the two of them, the way her mom once had.

After her mom ran away, Brynn feared her dad would

abandon her, too. For months, the constant worry had gnawed at her. If her mom hadn't loved her enough to stay, something must be wrong with her, and if something were wrong with her, how long would it be until her dad came to the same realization?

Desperate to make her dad happy and prevent him from abandoning her, too, Brynn had taken over many of the household chores. All the chores she hadn't done when her mom was around.

She handled the grocery shopping and the laundry, and at least once a week, she tidied up the house, dusted and ran the vacuum. On the weekends, she cleaned the pool and weeded the flowerbeds while her dad mowed the lawn. Every morning, she started her dad's coffee brewing and every evening, she made dinner.

But she'd never cooked for six people before and she had no clue how much she should make. Come to think on it, she had no idea what they even liked to eat.

Before she could overthink it, she decided their first home-cooked meal in their new country should be something classically American. But pizza delivery didn't seem to fit the occasion, so she opted instead for burgers and hot dogs, which meant she needed to make a quick run to the store at the end of their street.

She visited the small store often, even more so recently, since her dad had given her a credit card to use whenever she bought groceries or other household items, and she didn't mind the short walk. From the end of their driveway, it took her only nine hundred and eighty-eight steps to reach the store's front door.

Brynn often counted her steps and by now had designed all her most frequent trips so that she arrived at her destination on an even number, unlike the day her mom stopped coming home when she'd counted her steps for the first time and stepped through the front door of her school on an odd number. One-thousand, seven hundred and forty-three, to be exact.

When she returned home, she set to work readying heaping

bowls of potato salad and baked beans. Fearing it wouldn't be enough, she tossed together a massive fruit salad and boiled several ears of corn on the cob. In the freezer, she'd stashed a gallon of marble fudge ice cream for emergencies and mixed a pan of brownies to go with it for dessert later.

Before she'd had a chance to arrange the dining table, Rory and Cian appeared from their bedroom, drawn by the aromas. They hovered over her as she pulled the pan of brownies from the oven and plucked choice wedges of potato from the bowl, wolfing them down before she could hand either of them a fork.

To keep their fingers occupied and out of the food, she started passing them dishes and condiments to deliver to the table. By the time they'd finished laying out the feast, Brynn's dad and Siobhan had wandered inside from the back deck where they'd been talking and swaying on the old porch swing.

"Rory, go tell Aiden supper's ready, will ye?" Siobhan settled into the chair Brynn's dad had pulled out for her.

With a scowl, Rory shoved the serving spoon piled high with potato salad back into the bowl and pushed up from the table.

"Brynn, you made all this?" Siobhan seemed genuinely impressed, and a bloom of pleasure sprouted in Brynn's chest. "Everything looks—"

"Aiden, c'mon an' eat now!" Rory hollered from the top of the basement stairs.

Returning to his seat, Rory reclaimed the abandoned spoon and plopped a heavy glob of potato salad onto his plate.

When everyone had filled their plates, Brynn lifted her fork from the table, but before she could scoop up her first bite of fruit salad, Siobhan, Cian, and Rory bent their heads and simultaneously tapped their foreheads, sternums, and both of their shoulders. Then Rory muttered something about the Lord and blessings before wrapping up with a resolute "Amen," which Cian and Siobhan promptly repeated.

Then they ate.

Cautiously, Brynn raised the fork to her lips and bit into a sweet, ripe melon. When Aiden quietly emerged from the basement, she forgot to chew while he rounded the dining table and eased into the only remaining chair, across from her.

Warm brown eyes landed on her face for the briefest of moments before sweeping over the tabletop.

His mouth pulled down at the corners.

A ripple of uncertainty disturbed her. With a painful gulp, she swallowed. Had she made too much? Not enough? Didn't he like hamburgers? Or potato salad? Or chips or beans or store-bought bread? They were European, for crying out loud, not heathens accustomed to a crappy American diet. What had she been thinking?

She braced for his cruel comment.

He gaped at her. "Ye made all dis?"

Her throat tight, she nodded.

"Why?"

When she considered how pathetic the real answer sounded, she shrugged and stabbed a hunk of cantaloupe. "I was hungry," she mumbled.

Siobhan shot Aiden a pointed look. "Why don't ye just eat it." She offered Brynn a warm smile. "It's delicious."

"Wait 'til you try her baking," her dad said with a wink.

The delicate bloom of Brynn's pleasure wilted when Cian's menacing scowl reappeared, aimed, once again, at her dad.

Ignorant of the daggers being flung at him, her dad wiped his mouth with a napkin.

A light danced in his eyes when he regarded Siobhan. "Shall we tell them?"

"Tell us what?" Cian delivered each word with a stinging bite.

Siobhan pulled her gaze from Brynn's dad. "We're getting married."

"Yeah." Straightening, Rory leaned back in his chair. "We know."

"We're getting married next month," Siobhan said.

A blanket of displeasure stole over the boys.

"Ye said ye were goin' ta wait." Cian spoke through clenched teeth. "Dat's what ye told us."

"We *were* going to wait," Brynn's dad jumped in. "But after looking into it, we decided we want to get married before Aiden turns eighteen."

Alarm stole across Aiden's features. "What's dat got ta do wit anyting?"

"As long as your mother and I marry before your eighteenth birthdays, you'll be granted US citizenship."

Rory shifted uneasily in his chair. "We won't be able to go back home? To Ireland?"

"Of course ye will," Siobhan said softly. "You'll have dual citizenship. That way, ye can travel to both countries anytime ye like, as often as ye like."

"Ye do not have to do dat." Aiden's face had drained of color. He jabbed his fork in Siobhan's direction. "Yer marrying her. Not us."

"He wants to do it." Siobhan squeezed Brynn's dad's hand. "So we can be a family."

"That's how family works." Her dad's voice roughened. "At least, that's how this family is going to work. We take care of each other. We protect one another. No matter what."

Brynn had never heard her dad say such things before, and a jolt of alarm knocked into her.

Then the shadows swept suddenly from his expression. "Besides, I want you to be able to visit your mother anytime you like."

"What if ye get a divorce?" Cian challenged.

Rory elbowed him.

"No matter what happens between your mother and me, your citizenship status won't change. Unless you choose to change it, I suppose, and go through the legal hoops to do so, you'll remain citizens as long as you wish to be. The same way you'll be my sons," he said, the weight of the words lowering his voice, "unless or until you wish it otherwise."

Brynn watched varying degrees of shock and unease, along with an abundance of confusion, play across her stepbrother's features.

Though the frown remained on his face, Aiden dipped his head toward her dad.

Her heart jumped, as thrilled by the warm moment between he and her dad as she was by the sound of his deep voice when he said, *"Tank ye."*

The turn of events seemed to make the boys hungry, and the soft clash and clatter of utensils against dinner plates was the only sound in the room as they proceeded to consume more food than Brynn had imagined was possible to do in one sitting.

Right about the time she began to worry she hadn't made enough, Cian bounded up from the table. Shoveling the last bites of a burger into his mouth, Rory followed Cian into the kitchen. They dumped their empty plates beside the kitchen sink, then filed back to the table.

"Night, Ma." Cian dropped a kiss on the crown of Siobhan's head, then veered toward the front door.

"You boys be smart." Siobhan lifted her chin, and Rory's kiss landed on her cheek. "Use those big brains I've given ye."

The pair disappeared through the front door.

Dumbfounded, Brynn gaped at Siobhan. Wasn't she going to ask them where they were going? Or tell them what time to be home?

Apparently not, as Brynn's dad had already recaptured her attention. As dinner progressed, Siobhan's gaze kept returning to Brynn's dad, who eagerly anticipated every glance and stolen glimpse like a puppy awaiting his treat. The looks they exchanged communicated much without a single spoken word.

Brynn pretended not to notice. She stared at her plate and at the view of the pool through the patio doors. When she risked another glance at her dad and soon-to-be-stepmom, her dad was leaning in for a kiss... His mouth opened slightly...

Brynn jerked her head away.

Her gaze collided with golden brown eyes.

The smile playing on Aiden's lips matched the teasing light in his dark eyes.

With a soft sigh, Siobhan pushed up from her chair. "I'm going to go lie down. The jet lag has hit me hard."

Brynn perked up. She hadn't had a moment alone with her dad since yesterday, before they left for the airport. Maybe they could watch a movie together? She'd even let him pick and wouldn't complain when he chose one of those boring old war movies.

Just as she opened her mouth to suggest it, her dad placed his napkin on the table and stood.

"I think I'll join you," he said. "I've got a busy day tomorrow and could use a good night's rest."

Brynn swallowed back her disappointment. Guess her dad wouldn't be helping clear the table and clean the kitchen, a task they'd done together every other evening.

On the stairs, her dad caught up with Siobhan. His hand found her hip, and Siobhan's giggle ricocheted down the stairwell. Footsteps sounded overhead, and then the bedroom door closed with a resounding bang.

Her mind followed them a moment longer and, mildly repulsed, she scrunched her nose.

Aiden's low laugh rolled across the table.

Then he resumed his meal. He didn't rush to eat, or do the polite thing and ignore her existence. He looked right at her when his lips parted and a potato wedge disappeared inside his mouth. Slowly, he chewed. His throat worked when he swallowed.

Like the night before, she flushed with warmth. It was as

though his heat stretched across the table to lick her skin. Her heart pounded in her ears, and no matter how hard she tried not to look at him, her gaze kept wandering back to his face.

Upstairs, soft bumps and the faint sounds reached them through the floorboards.

One of his dark eyebrows quirked, just a hint of playfulness that coaxed a giggle from her.

He continued to eat without conversing while she pushed the last bites of food around on her plate, unable to fit them into her stomach with the butterflies banging against her insides.

When he'd emptied his plate, he rose slowly to his feet. He piled their parents' plates on top of his and carried the stack into the kitchen. At the sink, he ran water over the stack and loaded them one by one into the dishwasher while Brynn cleared the rest of the food from the table and packed the few remaining left-overs into containers.

When he'd eased the dishwasher door shut, he filched a dish-towel off the counter and dried his hands.

His gaze collided with hers. "Tank ye for dinner," he said softly, and she decided she adored the way he never made the *th* sound, pronouncing words like thank and this as tank and dis.

Turning, he crossed to the basement stairs and slipped through the door, thus ending their first meal together as a family.

BY THE THIRD week living with her new family, Brynn was thoroughly unsettled.

Stupidly, she'd assumed her stepmother would want to take over some, if not all, of the housework, but as it turned out, Brynn couldn't have been more wrong. Since arriving, Siobhan hadn't visited the grocery store once, and given the fact the boys ate like an army, Brynn had had to make several emergency trips to restock the cupboards. Neither had Siobhan done a single load of laundry or prepared even one meal, unless the few slices of buttered toast she made for herself each morning counted.

Indeed, Brynn's stepmother didn't seem all that interested in cooking or cleaning.

Or parenting, really.

Brynn's stepbrothers came and went as they pleased, often going out after dinner and not returning home until some unknown hour in the middle of the night. Even Rory, who was three years younger than Brynn, had stayed out well past midnight on several occasions. About that, Siobhan had little to say.

Nor did she utter a word when all three boys slept past noon, only to lounge by the pool or laze in front of the TV playing video games all afternoon.

With her sons either absent or asleep, Siobhan seemed to care only about spending time with Brynn's dad, and Brynn's dad seemed to care only about spending time with his soon-to-be wife.

No one cared to spend time with Brynn.

On the upside, there wasn't a lot of housework for Brynn to do. Her stepbrothers didn't own a lot of stuff, so they didn't leave a lot of clutter lying around, and they appeared not to want her touching their dirty laundry, as they took care of that task themselves. And while they happily devoured any food she set in front of them, they didn't seem to expect her to cook for them, a theory she decided to test that evening.

Rather than rush indoors to begin dinner preparations, she rolled over onto her stomach on the sun-warmed beach towel.

Beside her, Molly propped on her elbows to peer across the patio where Rory and Cian kicked a soccer ball back and forth.

"I still can't believe your dad is getting remarried," she said.

Molly lived only a few houses away, and although she attended an all-girls private school across town while Brynn went to the local public school, they'd been best friends since kindergarten and often spent their summers hanging out at Brynn's pool or at the country club where Molly's family were members.

"So?" Molly said. "What are they like?"

Countless descriptors rushed to Brynn's lips—*grouchy, scowly, hard, naked!*—but not one could she share with her friend. How did she explain that she'd lived in this house all her life and never once had it felt small or cramped, until now? That, though her stepbrothers were barely ever at home, she felt suffocated by their presence?

Because to admit that, Brynn would also have to confess her suspicion that if Aiden were the only newcomer in her home, she'd feel the same unnerving confinement.

"I don't know." Brynn rested her cheek on her forearm and frowned. "They're weird."

Molly shielded her eyes from the sun. "Really? Like how?"

"I don't know. They're boys."

"Yeah, boys are weird." Molly's gaze followed Aiden as he crossed the patio and, stepping onto the lawn, intercepted the ball Rory had booted to Cian. "They sure are cute though."

Squinting against the bright sun, Brynn followed her friend's gaze. "You think?"

"Hell yeah. You probably can't see it because they're your brothers, but they're freaking hot."

"They are not my brothers." Brynn couldn't suppress the denial.

Molly flicked her wrist. "Well, they basically are."

Later that week, Brynn and Molly had reclaimed their spots by the pool. The scents of chlorine and fresh-cut grass teased Brynn's nostrils, and the warm sun baked her skin, lulling her into drowsy apathy, when a soft, high-pitched sound disturbed her relaxation.

"Omigod," Molly hissed. "He won't stop staring at me."

"What?" Brynn lifted her head off the beach towel. "Who?"

But Brynn didn't need to wait for Molly's answer. Across the patio, beneath the shade of a maple tree, Aiden reclined in a lounge chair. Despite the book lying open in his lap, his gaze traveled across the sparkling pool and fixated on them. The hard scowl Brynn had grown accustomed to was stamped on his striking features.

"I think he likes me." Molly flipped her dark hair over one shoulder and adjusted her bikini top, a move obviously intended for Aiden's eyes. "Do you think he likes me?"

A pang struck Brynn beneath the breastbone. "I don't know..."

Molly lifted her face to the sun and arched her back, pretending not to notice Aiden while at the same time posing for him.

Brynn's head bobbed as she looked from her friend to Aiden and back.

Her stomach twisted with knots. Heat rushed to the surface of her skin, though not in the same pleasant way it did when *she* was the focus of Aiden's gaze. Furious warmth lashed her sensitive skin, and her heart beat so rapidly she feared it might burst.

She was jealous. Painfully, shamefully jealous. The envy as green as the emerald jewel-tone color of her bikini.

Unable to bear the fire of her envy, she clambered to her feet. The concrete patio burned the soles of her bare feet as she crossed to the edge of the pool and, without breaking stride, dove headfirst into the cool water.

The shock of cold rushed over her. Beneath the surface, she pushed through the waves, holding her breath as long as possible before kicking to the surface. When she emerged gulping for air, Aiden was walking across the patio toward the house.

She swam to the ladder and climbed out of the pool, but as she wrung the moisture from her long hair, a shiver of awareness prickled over her skin.

When she looked up, golden brown eyes ensnared her.

He'd paused at the patio door, one foot inside the house, and she froze, gripped by the fierce intensity of his gaze as it inched ever so slowly over her body.

Everywhere his eyes touched, her body reacted. She became hot and shivery at once. Her nipples hardened, and she knew without looking that they'd be visible beneath the wet, clinging fabric of her bikini top. The urge to conceal herself existed alongside the wanton desire to do something—anything—to maintain possession of his hungry gaze.

Except she had no idea how to hold the attention of a boy like Aiden, a fact that bore out a moment later when he turned and disappeared inside the house.

After that day, she didn't see him by the pool anymore.

CHAPTER 3

*B*rynn's dad married Siobhan in a small ceremony at a nearby Catholic church one Friday afternoon. Brynn stood at her dad's side, a sheen of moisture glistening on her skin as the tea-length, robin's-egg blue satin dress Siobhan had chosen for her provided little relief from the warm stifling air inside the church.

Across the aisle, the boys had taken their positions at their mother's side. Appearing cool and not at all sweaty, they wore matching scowls on their handsome faces as they looked on.

Though she fell into Aiden's direct line of sight, he didn't spare so much as a glance for her throughout the short ceremony.

Since that day at the pool, she'd failed to recapture his notice even once. It'd become an obsession. What could she do, or wear —or not wear—to make him look at her the way he had that day? But her efforts had proven futile.

Whenever she donned her emerald-green bikini, he disappeared, like a shadow vanishing in the sunlight.

When she'd borrowed a pair of shorts from Molly, shorts so short the material barely covered the swells of her bottom, and paired them with a dark purple tank top that brought out the green in her light eyes, he'd looked right past her as she paraded through the kitchen. As though she were invisible to him. Nothing but a ghost in skimpy clothing. Then he'd dumped his half-eaten sandwich in the kitchen trash and strolled toward the basement door.

A pang had lashed at her. What had she been thinking? Boys like Aiden weren't interested in girls like her. Mortification had stung her cheeks.

By the time Siobhan and her dad shared their first kiss as a married couple, a glum gray cloud colored Brynn's mood. What a fool she was, chasing after a boy who wouldn't talk to her, or even look at her.

Now, they were brother and sister.

At home after the ceremony, her dad and Siobhan retreated to the back patio with two glasses of wine. Watching from the kitchen window, Brynn wondered if she and her dad would ever experience another one of their quiet nights together hanging out by the pool or watching a movie.

When her dad laughed at something Siobhan said, then lifted their entwined hands to kiss her knuckles, Brynn turned away from the window.

In the living room, Aiden and Cian stood in front of the TV clutching black controllers, which they used to navigate the twists and turns of a winding video game racetrack. Behind them, Rory chided Cian when Aiden's racecar sneaked past his.

Moments later, a chorus of groans and jeering erupted when the game ended suddenly with Aiden's car seizing a close victory.

She stepped forward. "Can I play?"

Three heads swiveled toward her. The humor melted from Aiden's expression like an ice cube on the sun-drenched concrete patio outside.

"Here." He thrust his controller at her. "Ye can take my place."

Dropping the plastic device into her hand, he strode from the room.

She frowned down at the device, still warm from his touch.

"You want to be red or green?" Cian hit buttons on his controller, and the screen on the TV changed.

"Uh… green, I guess."

He reached over and pushed a button on her controller to select the green racecar. "Dat's yer gas pedal and dat one steers. Ready?"

"Ready."

Four seconds into the game, she drove her car into a blue pixelated lake.

With a low chuckle, Cian restarted the game. "Let's try dat again."

Her second attempt, she managed to complete the race, though she crossed the finish line in last place. Rory took Cian's controller for a turn, and by the end of their game, she started to get the hang of the touchy controls.

When the next game ended with her coming in second place, Rory shot her a side-eyed glance as he handed the controller back to Cian.

Her self-satisfied smile vanished when Cian pressed the button to begin their race. She bit down on her bottom lip and leaned right, then left, as she zigzagged through the difficult course. At the last second, Cian made an unexpected move to glide over the black-and-white checked strip a whisper ahead of Brynn.

All three of them were laughing when the patio door slid open and her dad stepped inside the house. A distinct chill infused the room while her dad retrieved the wine bottle from the counter and refilled one of the two empty wineglasses.

Brynn's stomach knotted.

Rory pressed the Start button. Their cars raced across the TV screen when she heard the slider door and knew her dad had returned outdoors.

Soon, she and Rory approached the final turn, but she didn't bother to try to slide her car through the small opening to pass Rory. "Why don't you like my dad?"

In silence, the race ended. Both boys avoided her gaze.

"Did he say or do something?" she asked

Rory looked down at the controller in his hand. "It's not yer da."

"It's our ma."

She faced Cian. "What do you mean?"

His clear hazel eyes clouded with uneasiness. "She has terrible taste in men."

"God awful." Rory switched off the television.

"Well, you don't have to worry." Brynn slid her controller into the case Rory held open. "My dad's not a bad guy. You'll see," she added when no one readily agreed with her.

"I guess we will."

A FEW NIGHTS LATER, Brynn's dad called her downstairs.

"We're going to watch a movie," he said. "Want to join us?"

Only minutes before, she'd stepped out of the shower and tossed on a lightweight cotton T-shirt and loose-fitting shorts. She did not want to watch a movie with her stepbrothers dressed in her pajamas, but neither did she want to disappoint her dad. He was trying to make them into a family, and whether he knew it or not, he faced an uphill battle.

She followed him into the living room, where he joined Siobhan on the couch. Stepping over Cian's long, stretched-out form on the floor and Rory's crossed ankles, she darted past Aiden, ducking to avoid blocking his view of the TV, and claimed the last seat in the armchair next to his.

Goosebumps prickled across her skin when she eased onto the chair's cool leather. Or maybe it was Aiden's warm gaze that caused her flesh to tingle.

His eyes lingered on her bare legs, then clamped on her flimsy pajama top. She wore no bra, having ditched the confining garment before bed, and his heated stare all but singed the flimsy cotton off her body.

Beneath her breastbone, her heart thrashed wildly.

From the couch, Siobhan laughed softly at something Brynn's dad had said but no one else could hear, and Aiden reacted to the quiet reminder of their parents' presence in the room as though a horn had blared. He jerked his head around and fixed his attention on the television screen.

Brynn tried to follow what was happening in the movie, but with Aiden sitting between her and the TV, her eyes kept wandering back to him.

She made a study of his profile. The elegant line of his straight nose. The angular shape of his strong jaw. The dramatic sweep of his heavy eyelashes. In her chest, a light airiness expanded. The act of simply gazing at him puffed happiness into her heart, like air into a balloon.

A balloon which Siobhan promptly burst.

"It's a lovely home," she said with her sweet smile and appealing accent. "But we might need something a little bigger, don't ye think?"

Brynn couldn't stem her gasp of pain. Siobhan wanted them to move?

Where would they go? Brynn had lived in this house her whole life. All she had left of the mother who abandoned her were her memories. Memories of her mom *in this house*. If they moved, would the memories go with her? Or would they stay behind, lost to her forever, just as her mom had been?

A crinkle of concern disturbed her dad's forehead. "I'm not sure we can afford a bigger home right now."

"Maybe not right now," Siobhan said easily. She slipped her hand inside of his. "But someday soon."

Her dad sipped his wine, his nose turning a touch redder with each swig. "If I sell that house on Leavitt Street, and the sale of the house in Ukrainian Village goes through this month, it might be possible."

Siobhan's smile was as warm as the summer sun when she kissed Brynn's dad on the cheek.

Brynn's stomach dropped to the floor. Suddenly averse to her dad's serene expression, she turned her face away.

To find herself the focus of a discerning, gilded gaze.

Aiden watched her closely, his expression inscrutable. Could he see that the thought of moving upset her? Did he know the thought of losing her home made her nauseated? Having just lost his home in much the same way, was he reveling in her misery?

In case, she lifted her chin and pasted a fake smile on her face. She'd be damned if she'd give him more fuel to loathe her.

THE FIRST DAY of a new school year arrived, bringing with it a break in the dark clouds of Brynn's mood. Not because she was happy to be starting back to school after summer vacation. She wasn't. She hated school.

Not the schoolwork necessarily, but as an awkward kid with massive self-esteem issues, high school was a certain kind of torture for Brynn. And despite the fact it was her last year, and she'd gotten her braces taken off the previous June, she didn't expect her senior year to be any better than the eleven before it.

Nonetheless, she was eager for any excuse to escape the house and the maddening torment of living with Aiden.

For the most part, he avoided and ignored her, but every once in a while, whenever they were forced to be in the same room together, she'd catch him watching her with a dark, intent scowl or feel his hot, searing gaze as it slipped slowly over her body. Every glance, every glimpse was a delicious agony that left her feeling hot and shivery, bold and uncertain, desired and loathed, all at once.

She lived for those rare, fleeting moments, and when they ended, she experienced the loss of his attention like a tiny, shattering death.

It was enough to make her crazy.

Her escape, however, was short-lived.

Dismay stabbed at her when Aiden slid into the seat one desk away from hers in fourth-period English Lit.

When Samantha Whitaker dropped into that empty seat between them, Brynn barely stifled a groan.

Sam flipped her long dark hair over one shoulder and hit Aiden with a wide smile. "You're new, aren't you?"

"That I am."

Her high-pitched squeal pierced Brynn's eardrums.

"OMG, I love your accent." She leaned forward, the motion pushing her boobs together and making them look bigger than they actually were. "Are you from Australia?"

"Crikey, you're right about that, mate," Aiden deadpanned.

The giggle escaped Brynn before she thought to stop it.

Sam's head snapped around and she pinned Brynn beneath a cold glare for one painful heartbeat. Then she turned back to Aiden.

"Some of us are going to the lake this weekend," she said. "You wanna come?"

Before Aiden could respond, the final bell rang and Mr. Strickland started class.

But Saturday morning, Aiden left the house with Cian and Rory well before noon and didn't return until late, his skin sun-kissed and his hair windblown, as though he'd spent the day on a boat in Lake Michigan.

It shouldn't have surprised Brynn that her stepbrothers would be popular at school. She expected that Aiden, a senior like Brynn, would be well-liked among their peers. But that Cian and Rory, a sophomore and a freshman, achieved a higher social status than she could ever imagine, rankled her fragile ego.

Monday in fourth period, Samantha gifted Aiden with a warm smile. An inviting smile.

A knowing smile.

The punch of envy left Brynn gasping for breath. Her jealousy wasn't green. It was darker, uglier, and it lashed out from someplace deep inside her. Someplace she didn't want to look. The place that harbored her darkest, most crippling insecurities.

Worse yet, Sam Whitaker wasn't the only girl to catch Aiden's eye. He flirted with them all. Every single day. Whether she was pretty or plain, popular or awkward, none escaped his effusive flirtations.

Except Brynn.

Thus, a month into the new school year, Brynn's tentative hope that this year might not be quite as horrible as all the others had faded and she was seriously considering asking her dad to send her to the all-girls school Molly attended across town.

The following Saturday morning, she woke up early so that she could talk to her dad before he left for work and ask him to do exactly that.

But when she got downstairs and caught her first real look at her dad in the last two days, she abandoned her mission.

Two puffy bags sat under his eyes and he stared off into space through half-closed eyelids. The exhaustion dragged at his shoulders, and she realized the reason she hadn't laid eyes on him in days was because he'd been putting in long hours at the office, staying late most evenings and working the weekends as well.

He'd been keeping crazy hours for weeks. Ever since Siobhan mentioned moving to a new house.

Brynn refilled his coffee cup and dropped a quick kiss on his cheek before heading upstairs to shower. She could talk to him later.

That evening, she fixed a huge pan of lasagna for dinner. Her dad's favorite.

Dinnertime came and went, without her dad. Rather than eat, Brynn kept the lasagna warming in the oven. She kept it warming for nearly two hours before he walked in the back door.

While Siobhan greeted him, Brynn pulled the pan from the oven and carried it to the table, then she fetched a cold beer from the refrigerator and set it at her dad's plate.

The boys, who had been on their way out the door, rushed to the table. Cian and Rory inhaled two huge slices each and then bounded up again.

In a rare display of parenting, Siobhan caught them before they escaped. "And where do ye think you're going?"

"Out." Cian shoved half a dinner roll into his mouth.

"There's a party up the street," Rory added and reached for the doorknob.

Aiden pushed up from his chair. "I'll keep an eye on 'em, Ma."

Siobhan waved for him to sit. "Wait for yer sister. She hasn't finished eating yet."

Brynn nearly choked on her water. All eyes landed on her.

"That's okay," she said. "You don't have to wait for me."

"Yes, they do." Siobhan gestured to the empty chairs, and her stepbrothers trudged toward them. "We cannot have ye going to that party alone."

Brynn blanched. "Oh, I'm not going."

Siobhan blinked at her. "Why not?"

Heat flushed Brynn's cheeks. "I, uh... I... have homework."

Siobhan waved a hand. "Ye have all day tomorrow to do that. Go out with your brothers. Have some fun."

"You should go," Brynn's dad said, his gaze lingering on Siobhan a tad too long and revealing far too much.

Brynn's mouth went slack. Was her dad trying to get rid of her?

With a hard clench, she set her jaw. "I don't want to."

Her dad waved off her protest. "Of course you do."

"What teenager doesn't want to go to a party?" Siobhan appeared truly baffled.

"Me," Brynn said.

Her dad and stepmom laughed, as though she'd made a joke.

But it wasn't a joke. Brynn's stomach turned over.

"Don't stay out too late," Siobhan told the boys.

"Have her home by eleven," her dad instructed them.

"Dad!"

"What?"

Brynn clutched her fork in her fist and stared at him, wishing the ground would open up and swallow her whole. That'd shut them up.

"I said I don't want to go."

A ripple of unease flitted across his face, and for a brief moment, she thought she'd finally gotten through to him.

Then, he shrugged. "Why not?"

"Because I wasn't invited."

Silence dropped like a loaf of unleavened bread. She could practically taste the tang of awkwardness in the room.

"The kids at school..." she lifted her shoulders and let them drop heavily, "...they don't like me all that much."

"They do not dislike you," Aiden said, his voice held a softness she'd never heard before. "It's only that they do not know ya."

"Ye should talk," Rory agreed.

"They'll like you just fine once they know ya a bit better," Cian added.

Brynn very much doubted that, but she was too relieved not be going to that party, and too shaken by the buttery warmth in Aiden's golden eyes, to argue.

Less than a week later, all had returned to normal, with Aiden ignoring her so completely she'd begun to doubt her own existence.

Friday in fourth period, Samantha's cackling laughter grated along Brynn's spine.

"Omigod, Aiden, you're so funny." Sam placed her ugly, red-tipped paw on his arm. "We should totally go out sometime. We'd have a blast."

As an easy smile worked its way across Aiden's lips, Brynn twisted abruptly in her seat, giving them her back.

In the seat next to her, Kyle Pierson looked up from his notebook at her sudden motion.

She gaped, unsure what to do.

You should talk more.

She smiled weakly. "Hi."

"Hi." He held out the stick of gum he'd just slipped from the pack. "Want one?"

Despite the fact that Mr. Strickland forbade chewing gum in his classroom, Brynn took the foil-wrapped treat and peeled away the paper.

"Thank you," she said, ducking her chin to pop the gum into her mouth without detection.

"You're welcome."

Kyle had a nice smile, she thought, returning her attention to the front of the classroom.

The next day, when she slid into her seat, Kyle offered her a smile, and she realized he was actually kind of cute. His hair was lighter than Aiden's and his eyes blue rather than brown, but still, he was handsome.

In his own way.

His nice smile made an appearance. "How's it going?"

"Good," she said. An awkward beat followed. "H-how's it going for you?"

His mouth quirked and he gave her a one-shoulder shrug. He

flipped over the paperback book on his desk. "Did you read the assignment?"

She nodded. "You?"

"Nah. Did I miss anything?"

She mimicked his shoulder shrug. "Only a world war and bunch of swear words."

"Really?" He spread the book's spine and fanned the pages.

"Really." His smile was infectious and spread to Brynn's face as Mr. Strickland started class.

Awareness prickled on the back of her neck and she looked up, then over.

Aiden, the dark scowl stamped on his face, lobbed golden-tipped daggers at her.

Her treacherous heart leapt, but she arranged her features into a placid mask and returned her attention to the front of the room.

THE WEEKEND BEFORE HOMECOMING, Brynn's dad poked his head inside her bedroom door. "Got a minute? Your mom and I want to talk to you."

A frown pulled at Brynn's mouth. Her dad had never referred to Siobhan as her mother before, and she couldn't help but wonder why he did so now. She rolled to a sitting position and climbed off the bed, where she'd been stretched out and working on a homework assignment for her chemistry class.

Downstairs, the boys sat lined up on the sofa while Siobhan perched on the edge of an armchair. Brynn's dad gestured to the other armchair, and Brynn sank down into it.

Her dad crossed to stand behind Siobhan and he placed his hands on her small shoulders.

Dread snaked through the pit of Brynn's stomach.

Craning her neck, Siobhan smiled up at Brynn's dad, then she shifted her gaze to her sons and a huge smile spread across her pretty face. "We're having a baby."

The slash of pain ripped through Brynn. *"What?"*

"It's true." Siobhan's cheeks flushed pink. "We didn't plan it. It just… happened."

A baby? But… but… but…

But Brynn was her dad's only child. For that reason, and likely no other, she was special to him. If he had a baby now, what did that mean for her?

Aiden leaned back, sinking more heavily into the sofa cushions, and Rory dragged a hand through his dark hair.

A pucker wrinkled Cian's brow. "Aren't ye a little old?"

Siobhan smacked him on the back of the head. "I am not old."

Brynn wanted to throw up, and she had no idea why.

Her dad and Siobhan were having a baby. A sweet, innocent baby.

She should be happy.

She didn't know what to think or feel, so all the thoughts and feelings pelted her at once. She tried to pick them apart, to understand the chaos swirling inside her, but every thread she unraveled led back to the same uncertain point.

Was she being replaced?

How would she fit into her dad's new family? Would she even have a place?

It was selfish and probably childish, but there it was.

Reaching up, Siobhan gripped Brynn's dad's hand. With a soft caress, she smiled up at him. "I hope it's a girl this time. I've always wanted a daughter."

The words landed like a punch to Brynn's gut, and a sharp puff of air shot from her.

Siobhan seemed to recognize her blunder and offered Brynn a weak smile. She held out her hand.

Dazedly, Brynn reached for it.

"We three will be the best of friends. You'll see." With a quick squeeze, Siobhan released Brynn's hand and stood.

After that, everyone filed out of the room, but Brynn remained in her spot, unable to move.

Unable to comprehend all that had suddenly, irrevocably changed.

CHAPTER 4

*T*hat night, the whole house slept while Brynn lay in her
bed staring at the ceiling in the dark.

Well, not all occupants of the house were asleep. Only those
inside the home at present slept.

Hours earlier, Rory and Cian had returned home after
another night out doing God knew what, and the muffled voices
in their bedroom had fallen silent some time ago. Aiden,
however, remained unaccounted for and was, presumably,
awake.

Somewhere.

Jealousy gnawed at her insides.

With a huff, she thrashed to her side, but the wall provided no
more interesting a view than the ceiling had.

She was tired, though she couldn't sleep. Tired of thinking
about him. Tired of contemplating who he was with and what
they were doing together. In the hours since she'd learned about
the baby, she'd already tired of worrying about her place in this
new family her dad was making for himself.

Despite her exhaustion, her mind wouldn't release her to
slumber. The thoughts spun around her brain, clunky and

uncomfortable, until one fleeting idea disrupted the torturous churn.

Ice cream.

On her most recent trip to the grocery store, she'd bought a huge tub of vanilla ice cream with chocolate fudge swirls, which she'd then stuffed behind the Brussel sprouts in the freezer. The decadent promise had her tossing back the covers and clambering from her bed at a quarter after two in the morning.

In the kitchen, she hauled the frozen tub from its hiding place and plopped it down on the kitchen counter. She scooped a heaping serving and settled on a barstool at the kitchen island. When she'd devoured nearly half the hearty helping, a sound at the back door gripped her.

She sat with the spoon buried between her lips when Aiden materialized from the dark night.

He drew up, and a veil of weariness crawled across his features.

Her stomach cramped. Must be exhausting, she thought dejectedly, harboring so much hate and dislike for her.

She stabbed at the suddenly unappealing mound of ice cream melting in her bowl. If she ignored him, maybe he'd vanish to his basement dwelling rather than hang out in her vile presence.

Except he didn't retreat downstairs.

The soft tread of his footfall drew near, then he stood before her. Reaching out, he pulled the spoon from her mouth, his unsettling gaze tracking the unhurried silver glide.

His lips parted slightly with his shortened breaths.

Without so much as a "hey, how are ya doing?" he eased open the cabinet drawer, selected a utensil, and carved out a bite of ice cream from her dish. When he slipped the spoon into his mouth, a small, almost imperceptible hum vibrated in the back of his throat.

He took another taste, and then, because she didn't know what else to do, so did she.

In the quiet of the night, they took turns choosing morsels from her bowl while beneath her lashes, she snuck glances at him, searching for clues about where he might've been.

His dark hair was rumpled, but there was nothing particularly unusual about that, and the wrinkles in his cotton T-shirt were ever-present. She sucked in a deep breath, sniffing for the scent of Samantha Whitaker's sweet perfume.

She smelled tangy citrus and fresh pine with a hint of the body soap she'd bought last week at the store. He smelled good, the way he usually did. Like Aiden.

Only Aiden.

The knot her heart had twisted itself into eased a little.

But as the large serving of ice cream shrunk to a tiny lump, his dark eyes made a study of her face.

She ducked her chin.

"You're not happy about the baby," he said.

Her heart thrashed against her ribcage. "Of course I am." Straightening, she shoved the bowl away. "I know you think I'm a terrible person, but I'm not that awful."

A pucker formed between his dark eyebrows. "I don't think that."

"Yeah, okay." She rolled her eyes. "Whatever you say."

His frown deepened.

Wielding her spoon, her hand sliced through the air. "You know, the polite thing would be to pretend you don't hate me and just talk bad about me behind my back. It's the way we do things here in America."

His mouth quirked. "Except I don't hate you."

"You act like I don't exist," she grumbled.

"Believe me," he said softly, "I see you."

Her heart seized, then tripped into a wild rhythm. "This is the first time you've talked to me in, like, forever."

"You mean with my clothes on?"

Heat rushed into her face and swept across her skin, raging like a wildfire.

In response, a smile lifted one corner of his mouth. "I didn't know you wanted to talk."

She lifted one shoulder. "I don't."

He leaned more deeply into the counter. "What would you like to talk about?"

"Where were you tonight?" The question burst from her.

"Out," he said after a telling beat of hesitation. Then, before she could demand who with, he pivoted. "What happened to your mom?"

She sucked a sharp hiss of air between her teeth. Shock and pain nearly knocked her off the barstool, and she gripped the edge of the counter.

Lies piled in her throat. Since her mom ran off, the lies had been Brynn's security blanket. Because she didn't understand what was so wrong with her that her own mother couldn't love her, she didn't know what she should and shouldn't reveal about herself to others. So she lied. Compulsively. Often, and about minor, unimportant things, such as her favorite color or what she'd eaten for lunch.

But now, the lies choked and gagged, and her mouth couldn't form the words that'd release them.

He watched her closely. "Did she and your dad divorce, then?" he asked gently.

Beneath his scrutiny, the falsehoods dissolved. For first time in years, deception wasn't an option. Not with Aiden.

There really wasn't any point lying to him anyway. He probably already knew the truth, if not from his mom, then surely Samantha Whitaker had filled him in on the gory details.

She dragged a shuddering breath into her lungs and released it. "She left."

The hard set of his features had softened. "Where did she go?"

"I don't know. She was supposed to pick me up from school,

but… she never showed up." The words hung in the space between them. "It was dark by the time my dad came for me."

His eyes stalked her. "How old were you?"

"Twelve."

A week later, she'd gotten her first period, and the two events were forever linked in Brynn's mind. By then, Samantha Whitaker, whose mom worked in the principal's office, had blabbed to the entire school that Brynn's mother had run away, leaving her daughter and husband with no word of her whereabouts.

Misery that her mom was gone and never coming back had turned to shame.

"You don't know where she is?" The softness in his voice pulled her away from the painful memories.

She shook her head.

"I'm sorry."

She managed a weak smile. "At least my dad's still here."

With his sharp scowl, she considered how pathetic that sounded.

"What about you?" She lifted the lid to the ice cream off the counter and fastened it onto the tub. "Did your mom and dad divorce?"

"They were never married." An edge cold enough to freeze ice cream crept into his voice.

She wondered about it. Was he angry he was stuck here while his dad was an ocean away? "Do you miss him?"

"Not at all."

"Don't you like him?"

"I don't know. He never said more than a few words to me when I'd catch him sneaking out me ma's bedroom." He hitched one shoulder. "I don't even know who he is."

Brynn's throat ached. "But… your mom knows, doesn't she?"

"She knows." Over his abdomen, he folded his arms. "She

cursed us with the bastard's last name, fer God's sake. Dat's all we know about him. His last name."

"Well, have you asked her who he is?"

"I have not."

She blinked at him. "Aren't you curious?"

"I am not." Emotion churned in his dark eyes. "He didn't want anything to do with us, and that's all I need to know about him."

Beneath Aiden's anger, Brynn detected a note of anguish. It was faint, and he did an admirable job of hiding it, but she was far too familiar with that soul-crushing grief not to recognize it in another.

Her chest squeezed. God, how it hurt, knowing that the people who should've loved you most in the world, more than anyone else and without condition, couldn't be bothered to be present in your life.

"I'm *so* sorry," she whispered.

Surprise flickered across his face, then in a rush of activity, he scooped the empty bowl off the counter and twisted away from her.

His back to her, he rinsed the bowl under a spray of water from the faucet. "Don't be sorry. We're better off without him."

She lugged the tub of ice cream to the refrigerator and slid it into the freezer. Turning, she let the door fall shut.

"Tank ye for the ice cream." He dried his hands on a towel. "I was starved."

"Didn't you eat when you were out?" It was shameless, she knew, but she couldn't keep the probing question inside.

His dark eyes glittered but offered her nothing.

"Fine, you don't want to tell me." She pretended immense boredom. "But I should warn you, Samantha Whitaker is not a nice person. She'll make a terrible girlfriend."

"I'm not looking for a girlfriend."

Brynn's shoulders slumped. So it was just sex, then. She didn't think it was possible to feel worse.

"I'm looking for—" Biting off the words, he tossed the towel on the counter.

"What?" she asked, her heart in her throat. "What are you looking for?"

He took so long to answer, she thought he would blow her off again.

Then, quietly, he said, "The One."

She pulled a face. "Seriously?"

Soft laughter rumbled in his chest. "Yeah, seriously."

Suspicious, she narrowed her eyes at him. "I didn't know guys our age were into that sort of thing."

"I'm not like the other guys."

Boy, was that an understatement. "So, what is it you're looking for? Besides gorgeous and stacked, that is."

"It has nothing to do with her looks. It's a feeling."

Her mouth went dry, and she licked her lips. "What kind of feeling?"

For a long moment, he gazed at her, and a terrible, gutting heartbreak came into his eyes. "I'll know it when I find her."

With that, he pushed away from the sink.

At the basement door, he stopped, and turned suddenly. He opened his mouth, as if he would speak, then his jaw snapped shut and he twisted away again.

Unable to catch her breath, she could only watch as he slipped through the door.

Two days later, Brynn ducked past Aiden as he and Alyssa Jensen lingered outside Mr. Strickland's classroom.

She tried to keep her gaze averted, but from the corner of her eye, she glimpsed Alyssa's hand on his arm, bare skin against bare skin, and her stomach roiled. In his voice, the low huskiness when he teased Alyssa that she would make him tardy for class sent Brynn's heart plummeting to her toes.

She plunged down the row of desks and dropped into her assigned seat.

Looking up from his cell phone, Kyle offered her a smile. "Hey."

"Hey," she said.

He shoved his phone into his pocket and twisted in his seat. "You going to the game Friday?"

That weekend, the school's football team would host a neighboring rival for their annual homecoming game. Never once had Brynn attended homecoming or any other high school football game.

"I'm still thinking about it," she lied.

"C.J. and I are going with some others. Do you want to come with us?"

Surprise and terror wrestled in her throat. "I… uh… I…."

"I'll pick you up." He held out a stick of chewing gum. "Say, around seven?"

Second bell rang and just as Mr. Strickland reached out to pull the door shut, Aiden slipped through it.

With a smile, Brynn accepted the gum from Kyle. "Yeah, okay."

She faced the front of the classroom, but she couldn't hear a word of Mr. Strickland's lecture over the shrill screeching inside her skull.

Had Kyle Pierson just asked her out?

It was only a football game, and he'd invited her along as part of a group with his friends, but she'd never been asked out by a boy before, even casually.

Laughter built in her throat, and she glanced around the classroom, wondering if the world had just suddenly upended for everyone else, too.

But no one seemed to notice that Brynn Hathaway had ceased to be a social outcast. Indeed, no one seemed to notice her at all.

Except Aiden. From his seat two rows over, he glowered.

She ignored him.

By Friday night, her excitement at being asked out had morphed into a nervous, nauseating dread in the pit of her stomach.

Why had she agreed to go out with Kyle and his friends? She barely knew them, and she had nothing in common with boys. What would they talk about? What if she said something stupid? What if she didn't say anything at all? Would they think she was weird or stupid, or both?

Locked in her bedroom, she tried to assemble an outfit similar to something Samantha or Alyssa might wear, but every combination she fashioned appeared more ridiculous than the last. After attempting fourteen different ensembles, she finally settled on a pair of dark wash blue jeans and a black sweater that hugged her torso.

As she tied the laces of her white Keds, the doorbell's chime rang throughout the house.

Her pulse skittering, she scurried downstairs, taking the steps two at a time. She darted by Aiden and Rory, who were ensnared by a video game, and leapt past Cian as he backed toward the door, his attention gripped by the combat playing out on the large television screen.

Breathing hard, Brynn yanked open the front door.

Kyle flashed his easy smile and stepped inside the house.

"Hey," he said. "Wow. You look great."

Pleasure warmed her cheeks. No one had ever complimented her looks before. "Thanks."

A blaring noise from the TV marked the video game's sudden end.

"Ha," Rory erupted. "Take dat, ye bastard."

Aiden ignored his brother's taunts. His spine rigid, he affixed his menacing scowl on Kyle Pierson, resembling a missile locked on its target.

Kyle leaned close. "You, uh, ready to go?"

Dragging her eyes away from Aiden, Brynn smiled up at Kyle. "Give me one sec. I'll grab my coat."

She dashed up the stairs, and in her bedroom, underwent a brief but frantic search for her wool jacket. Snatching it from underneath the pile of her discarded clothing, she rushed toward the door.

But as she passed by the mirror, she noticed that her fine hair had already started to fall flat, so she squirted hairspray onto the loosely coiled locks. Then she swiped another layer of lip gloss across her mouth before she hurried back downstairs, her jacket in hand.

But when she stepped into the living room, a heavy silence charged the air. As though all the oxygen had been sucked out of the room.

Dread lifted the hairs on the back of her neck. "Where's Kyle?"

No one answered her.

She looked to each of her stepbrothers, then zeroed in on Cian, who couldn't quite stifle his shit-eating grin.

"What's so funny?" she asked.

Cian's laughter broke loose, prompting a soft snicker from Rory.

Trepidation spiraling through her, Brynn shifted her gaze to Aiden.

No traces of humor were evident on his face. Not a hint of emotion could be found in his dark expression. Instead, he regarded her with a stoic, almost blank, stare.

Her throat squeezed. "What did you do?" she whispered.

CHAPTER 5

*A*iden shrugged. "Kyle had to go," he said, appearing bored with the conversation.

"He left?" She hated the hitch in her voice. "Why?"

"Because you are not going out with Kyle Pierson." The gold flame in his eyes matched the lick of fire in his tone.

"What? Why not?"

A muscle ticked along his jawline.

"If you can't give me a reason—"

"Because I forbid it."

She sputtered her outrage. "That is not your decision to make."

"Too late. He's gone." He dropped into an armchair and propped his feet on the coffee table. "And he's not coming back."

The blood in her veins went cold. "What did you say to him?"

He avoided her gaze.

She twisted toward Rory. "What did he say? Tell me. Please."

Guilt riddled Rory's expression. "He told Kyle you weren't feeling well enough to go out tonight." His gaze darted to Aiden, then away. "That you were... in the bathroom."

She frowned at Aiden. "You told him I was sick?"

All three boys took a sudden interest in the floorboards.

"But he just saw me. He knows I'm not throwing up."

Cian's soft snicker rankled. "No one said you were puking."

"Then what…?"

Cian lost the battle with his stupid grin. "The other end."

Brynn recoiled. "*What?*" She whirled on Aiden. "Why did you do that?"

His upper lip curled. "You don't even like him."

"Yes, I do. He's—he's—he's nice to me."

"He's a gobshite."

"I don't even know what that means." Heat scalded her face. "How dare you. You had no right."

In a flurry of motion, Aiden gained his feet and stalked toward her. "I had no right?"

"None." She refused to yield ground to him.

"I am your goddamn family." He pushed into her space.

"So what?"

Their bodies nearly touching, he put his face close to hers. "So, Kyle Pierson is a fecking tool with too high an opinion of himself."

Aiden's incredible scent overwhelmed her senses, and a scream of frustration piled in her throat. "You don't even know him."

"I know enough." His lashes swept down, and his gaze latched onto her mouth.

Her heart seized.

Warmth from his soft breaths danced across her sensitive skin. "Does he turn you on?"

Her chest rose and fell with her fury. She floundered for words.

His smile turned smug. "I didn't think so."

He eased his big body away and turned his back on her.

The breath she'd been holding flooded her lungs. "So you get to sleep with every girl in school, but I can't even go to a football game with a friend? Is that it?"

"Yes."

"Screw you."

He tossed a look at her over his shoulder. "All right, but I'll ruin you for every limp-dick preppy you try to take to your bed."

Her vision blurred with her brimming tears. "You are such a jerk."

Dark eyes bored into her. Through her. "You don't know the half of it."

The peal of the doorbell rang out, and she started.

With a sharp tug, Aiden yanked open the front door, and Alyssa Jensen materialized on a cloud of cloying perfume.

She offered Cian and Rory an overly bright smile. "Hi, guys." Her smile dimmed seductively when she turned it on Aiden. "Hi, you."

Aiden dipped his head close. "Can you give me a minute?" His gentle, reassuring tone gutted Brynn. "I'll be right out."

"Sure." Her smile stiff, Alyssa gave Brynn a cool once-over. "Meet you outside."

The moment the door closed, Brynn snapped. "Let me guess. Is she The One?"

A shadow chased across Aiden's face. He retrieved his jacket where he'd slung it over the back of an armchair.

Bitter laughter tasted sour on Brynn's tongue. "If all you're going do is fuck her, what does it matter?"

He pulled up. "It matters."

Months of hurt and anger, and maddening confusion, welled up. She wanted to scream and cry and kick something really hard. She wanted to lash out, to hurt him the same way he'd hurt her. At her sides, she balled her hands into tight fists and tried to hold the agony inside her.

She failed. "You're pathetic."

He ignored her and pushed his arms through the sleeves of his coat.

"You're never going to find her. This perfect girl you've created in your mind. She doesn't exist." Brynn couldn't stop the flow of stupid words pouring out of her mouth. Out of her heart. "None of these girls are ever going to love you."

Not the way I could.

The words were meant to wound him, but they boomeranged and pierced her heart instead. What if she was the one nobody would ever love? What if Kyle had been her one and only shot at happiness?

She gulped for air, struggling to catch her breath against the rush of terror-pain.

She wasn't completely naïve. She knew Kyle Pierson didn't love her. Not now. But he was the only boy who had ever shown any interest in her. What if he was the only boy who might have grown to love her one day?

And Aiden had ruined her chances with him.

Ruined her chances of ever finding love.

She would forever be Brynn Hathaway.

Unwanted.

Unloved.

Unlovable.

"You bastard." Pain roughened her voice. "No woman could ever love someone like you."

Her words hurt him. The pain she'd caused was visible on his face, in the way he held his head and the slight pinch at the corner of his mouth.

In his dark, turbulent eyes.

"You may be right about that," he said.

Unable to bear the moment any longer, Brynn ran from the room. She slammed her bedroom door and flung her body across the bed. Her face buried in a pillow, she let loose a primal scream.

She hated him. She hated what he'd done, and she hated that

watching him leave with Alyssa wounded her far more deeply than missing out on a date with Kyle Pierson.

Voices outside drifted through her bedroom windows. Two car doors banged shut, then a car engine fired.

That night, Aiden would be with Alyssa, and there was nothing she could do to stop him.

There was nothing she could do to make herself stop caring who he spent his nights with.

No matter that he was her brother now.

No matter that he cared so little about her that he'd ruined her chance with Kyle only to be cruel.

For the second time that night, her own words came back to injure her—she was the pathetic one, obsessing over a boy who thought so little of her.

Not just any boy, but her stupid, heartless, evil stepbrother.

Into her pillow, she emptied her tears.

THE THREAT of fourth period loomed over Brynn as she trudged through the front entrance of their high school on Monday morning. At her locker, she dumped her backpack on the bottom shelf and rifled around for her chemistry textbook.

What would she say to Kyle when she saw him? What would he say to her?

Her stomach heaved. The whole thing made her sick. Actually physically ill.

That, too, was Aiden's fault. He'd planted gross thoughts in her head and now—

She slammed shut her locker and gasped. "Kyle, uh, hi."

"Hi." A bemused smile played on his handsome face. "So what happened to you Friday?"

"Nothing!" The word burst from her at an almost-shout. "Nothing happened. Nothing at all."

One of his light eyebrows inched upward.

"It was—my stepbrothers, they...." She cringed. "They think they're funny."

His smooth laughter calmed her churning stomach. "I figured it was something like that."

"I'm so sorry. I—"

"It's okay."

She hugged the textbook to her chest. "Are you sure?"

"I have two older brothers. They can be real jerks."

"Boy, can they."

"See you in class," he said, backing away.

"See you." She chewed her bottom lip a moment. "I really am sorry."

"Don't worry about it." He flicked his wrist and a silver flash flew through the air.

She bobbled the foil-wrapped stick of gum before reeling it in.

In fourth period, she angled her body in her seat, preferring Kyle's bright good looks to Aiden's brooding darkness.

She no longer cared who Aiden flirted with, or what he thought of her. Or Kyle. Or her and Kyle together.

She didn't understand why Aiden hated her so much, or why he'd lied and said he didn't when clearly, he did, but she refused to care any longer.

Doing so hurt too much.

After school, she holed up in her bedroom and attacked the stack of college applications the school counselor had given her. That was how desperately she wished to avoid Aiden.

When the house had fallen quiet, hunger lured her from her hideout. Her stomach grumbling, she crept downstairs, but drew up to find Rory at the dining room table, hunched over a bowl of cereal.

She retrieved a bowl from the kitchen cupboard and filched a spoon from the drawer before she settled in a chair across from him at the table.

Tipping the box of cereal, she filled her bowl high with fruit-flavored puffballs. "Everyone asleep?"

His slow smile pulled up the corners of his mouth. "Cian will be up for a bit yet. He tinks he can beat me high score."

Soft laughter bubbled up as she loosened the cap on the milk jug. Had she gotten used to their accents, or had their melodic inflections eased since they'd moved to Chicago?

"And Aiden?" She poured milk into her bowl. "Is he still up?"

Rory chewed, then swallowed thickly. "He's out."

The stab of jealousy was agonizing, even if completely predictable. "Of course he is," she muttered.

Warm brown eyes that reminded her of Aiden's flickered over her.

"He must really hate being here." With her spoon, she speared her cereal, drowning brightly-colored puff balls in milk. "I mean, he's never home. Like, ever."

Rory crunched in silence.

"It's like he can't stand to be anywhere near us." She halted her assault on the cereal. "I mean, what is up with that?"

Unease played over his face. "Um…?"

She gazed into warm brown eyes untainted by disdain.

"Why doesn't he like me?" she asked, her throat tight.

Panic flooded Rory's expression.

Her cheeks on fire, she rushed to add, "I mean, not, like, *like* me, like me. But, like, why does he hate me so much?"

He frowned. "Did he say that?"

"No. But it's pretty obvious."

"Is this about the ting with Kyle?"

She stabbed an orange ball. "And other stuff."

"What other stuff?"

"Well." She shifted in her chair. "He's always frowning at me."

"He frowns at everyone." Rory shoveled another spoonful of cereal into his mouth. "Dat's just the way he looks."

"And the thing with Kyle."

"Dat had more to do with Kyle than you."

"He doesn't like Kyle?" Her jaw slackened. "Why not?"

Rory's shoulders moved. "Kyle's a gobshite."

"Okay, what does that mean?"

"You know, a geebag. A bollix."

She shrugged.

"Never mind." He pushed to his feet.

"No, I want to know." She twisted in the chair, following him as he carried his bowl to the kitchen sink. "Maybe he isn't as cool as you guys are, but—"

He shook his head. "Dat's got nothing to do with it."

"Then what?"

She waited while he finished rinsing the bowl. Deep lines bracketed his eyes and mouth, making him appear even more like his oldest brother, as he loaded the bowl in the dishwasher and used the heel of his foot to kick the door shut.

He careened toward the stairs.

"Rory?"

One foot on the bottom step, he glanced back at her over his shoulder. "Ye have to ask Aiden."

CHAPTER 6

*A*fter two weeks of self-imposed exile, Brynn was restless. And hungry.

She wanted something more substantial than a bowl of cereal or one of the granola bars she'd stashed in her dresser drawer. She wanted to escape her bedroom. Escape the house.

Escape her life.

Early one Saturday afternoon, she called Molly and invited her friend to the movies, but Molly already had plans with some girls from her school.

For approximately one-half of a second, Brynn considered going to the movies alone. But what if she ran into kids from school? If they saw her there alone, would they think she had no friends? That she was too big of a loser to find even one person who would want to go to the movies with her? Which was actually kind of the truth.

If the other kids knew the truth about her, what would they do? Would they laugh at her? Look down on her? Despise her?

The way Aiden did.

She rejected the idea and plucked a book off her shelves instead.

Curling up on the bed, she cracked open the spine. Since she'd first read it a couple of years ago, the book had been one of her favorites, and she quickly became lost in the pages of the sweeping romance.

She was so absorbed in the story, she almost didn't hear the car back down the driveway and pull away from the house when Aiden left.

Brynn bounded off the bed. She shot from her bedroom like a felon freed from her prison cell. Under her arm, she tucked her mom's old cookbook and made a mad dash for the kitchen, anxious to try her hand at the chicken casserole.

During her self-imposed isolation, Brynn had discovered the cookbook on her shelves and spent several days flipping through its worn pages, remembering what she still recalled of the mom that didn't want her. It struck Brynn to realize that her happiest memories of her mom, a woman prone to episodes of anger and melancholy, had taken place in the kitchen, where her mom often let Brynn help her cook.

Smells began to fill the house, and soon after, bodies began to appear. Rory snagged a hunk of cheese off the cutting board and disappeared upstairs. When Cian materialized at her shoulder, she slid a saucer piled with cheese wedges and chunks of cooked chicken across the island. He settled on a barstool and dragged the plate over.

The arrival of fall brought crisp temperatures and shortened days, and by the time the entire family minus Aiden filled in around the dining table, darkness blanketed the sky.

In the soft light from the chandelier overhead, Siobhan's black hair shimmered. "Any offers on the Mitchell house?"

With a heavy sigh, Brynn's dad shook his head. "Not one."

"I thought you said it's in one of the most popular neighborhoods in Chicago."

"The house needs a lot of work," her dad said, more worried than she recalled him sounding in years. "The owners don't want to drop the price, and most buyers aren't interested in a fixer-upper."

"Who'd want to buy a crappy house?" Rory snagged a roll from the breadbasket.

"Not many people, actually." A faint smile briefly chased away the frown lines on her dad's face. "I've tried to convince them to do some renovations, but they don't have the means."

"How much would it cost?" Brynn asked.

"It wouldn't be cheap, that's for sure, but they'd earn their money back on the resale two, maybe three times over."

Siobhan's dark eyes went wide. "Is that right?"

"Oh yeah. It really is a great neighborhood." Her dad scooped a second serving of casserole onto his plate. "It's not far from downtown, but far enough to get a decent-sized yard. And it has parking."

"What kind of renovations are needed?" Siobhan sipped from her water glass.

"Mostly cosmetic stuff. They need to paint all the rooms and replace the carpet, and the kitchen and bathrooms haven't been updated in decades." Her dad reached for a roll. "If they could do the work themselves, they'd save a ton of money, but they're an older couple and they both work in the city." Shaking his head, he lifted his shoulders. "It's simply too much for them."

"Maybe you could do it." The words popped out of Brynn's mouth.

Her dad frowned. "Do the renovations?"

"It's not a bad idea," Siobhan said. "Would your brother help?"

Brynn's uncle, a contractor who owned his own company with two friends from high school, specialized in home repairs and renovations.

"It'd be a lot of money up front, and a lot of work." Her dad wasn't frowning anymore.

"If there's any demolition involved, count me in." Cian pushed to his feet.

"I know dat's roy." As he stood, Rory filched two more rolls from the plate. "Put us down for breakin' stuff."

"I can help, too." Brynn straightened in her chair. "Do you need a spreadsheet? I have a class project due at the end of the year. Maybe I could track supplies or expenses for you?"

"That'd be great, sweetheart." The warmth from her dad's first full-fledged smile spilled over her.

"Where're you boys off to?" Siobhan craned her neck to peer up at Cian as he skirted behind her chair.

"To a friend's house up the street," Rory said.

Cian tipped his chin at Brynn. "Wanna come with us?"

Casserole lodged in her throat.

Rory tossed Cian a roll. "It should be the *craic*."

Brynn swallowed painfully. "I don't do crack."

For some reason, that was hysterically funny to them.

Siobhan waved a hand at her. "Go with your brothers, dear." She sent a soft smile across the table to Brynn's dad. "Make her go. She does so much around here. She deserves to have a night out with her friends."

"I don't have friends," Brynn stated.

Your oldest son made sure of that, she thought, stabbing at a chunk of chicken on her plate.

The concerned pucker reappeared on her dad's forehead. "It's a little late to go out."

"Yes, it is." Brynn jumped on the excuse, lame as it was considering the time hadn't yet reached seven o'clock. "It's way too late."

"But you know what? Your mother's right." He lifted his glass of wine off the table. "You deserve a break. You should go, honey."

"I don't want to."

But Cian was already pulling her chair out from under her. "It's time we did a little sibling bonding, don't ye tink?"

"No, I do not 'tink,'" she snapped.

He dumped her out of the chair.

With a yelp, she stumbled forward.

Rory shoved her coat at her. "We should've done this weeks ago."

"I'm not even dressed."

"Ye look grand." Unmoved by her protests, probably because she wore the same blue jeans and baggy sweater to school all the time, Cian hustled her out the door.

Cold night air smacked her in the face. She shoved her arms inside her coat and tugged the warm wool tight around her body as Cian and Rory set off down their quiet street.

Tagging along behind them, Brynn yanked the rubber band from her hair and let down the messy bun she'd piled on top of her head. She combed her fingers through the snarled strands while stumbling to keep up as they cut through the park.

They emerged on Longwood Drive. Nervous butterflies collided in her stomach. She'd never been to a house party before and had no idea what she'd find inside the two-story brick home. At the second crossroad, they turned off, and the muffled sound of loud music carried down the street. Four houses passed before they arrived at the source of the pumping beat.

Rory pushed open the front door and thumping music spilled out onto the porch. She stepped inside and was immediately enveloped.

Clusters of people hung out in small, scattered groups, their faces obscured by the dim lighting. She trailed Cian and Rory into the home's interior, and as they passed by pockets of people, she began to pick out the familiar faces of kids from her school.

In the dining room, a crowd packed around the table, playing a card game, and Cian peeled off to amble over.

Brynn followed Rory into the kitchen where the countertops were loaded down with red plastic cups and bottles of liquor. After a quick study of the bottles littering the island, Rory pulled open the refrigerator door.

He held out a can of beer to her. "Do ya drink?"

She'd never drank alcohol before in her life, but a quick glance around confirmed her suspicion that she'd be the only one not partaking if she refused.

Rory leaned close. "Ye can just hold on to it if ye want. No one will notice if you're not drinking it." With a wink, he pulled the tab and handed her the can.

From across the room, someone called out his name.

He lifted his hand and barked out a greeting, then twisted around to pluck another beer from the fridge. Before the refrigerator door eased shut, his friends had descended on them.

Brynn didn't know the names of the four guys who squeezed in around them, though she recognized their faces from the hallways at school. Each of them offered her a nod or a friendly smile when Rory introduced her, then they fell into an animated conversation about a movie they'd been to see earlier in the day.

From there, their conversation veered in many directions. Growing warm, she slipped out of her coat and hooked it over her arm while she listened. Mostly, the boys told ridiculous or outlandish stories and she soon found herself laughing along with them.

Rory, her quiet, unassuming stepbrother, spoke with colorful language and wild gestures, and was far and away the most entertaining of the bunch, which was saying a lot.

When a group of girls filed through the kitchen, Brynn pressed her back to the wall to make room for them to squeeze past.

"Hey, Brynn," one of them said.

Surprise caught and held Brynn's tongue a moment. "Hey, Brittany," she finally said.

She'd lost the thread of Rory's conversation with his friends, but it didn't matter. With a jolt, she realized she was at a house party attended by a bunch of kids from school, kids she'd known for years but never talked to, and she wasn't in misery.

She was having fun.

Just then, someone crashed into her with enough force to knock her against the wall.

"I'm sorry, sweetheart," a male voice purred. "I didn't even see you there."

She jiggled her hand, shaking off the beer that'd sloshed from her can.

"Brynn?"

At the sound of Kyle's voice, Brynn's head snapped up. "Kyle? Wh-what are you doing here?"

She cringed at the stupidity of her question.

"Just hanging out." He placed a hand on the wall beside her head, as if to steady himself. "I didn't expect to see you here tonight."

The guy who'd crashed into her, C.J., smacked him on the arm. "C'mon, man, let's go."

"Hold on a second." Kyle peered hard into her face. "I'm going to talk to Brynn for a minute."

C.J. gave her a long look while he took a slow, deep swallow from his Solo cup, then he dragged the back of his hand across his mouth. "I'll catch you later."

"Brynn Hathaway." Kyle sounded funny, like his tongue was swollen and too big for his mouth. "I can't believe you're here."

His light eyes bleary, his intense study of her face felt overly intimate. Invasive.

Her anxiety returned with a rush. Without thinking, she took a sip from the can of beer in her hand, and the bitter flavor flooded her mouth. She winced.

"What's wrong?"

She shook her head, unable to speak with her mouth full of foul beer.

"Is it the beer?"

She squeezed her eyes shut and gulped. "Oh, God, yes," she croaked. "It's awful."

Kyle's deep chuckle coaxed a self-mocking laugh from her.

He plucked the can out of her hand. "Hold on."

Weaving through bodies, Kyle worked his way across the cramped kitchen. He abandoned her beer on the counter by the sink and lifted a red Solo cup off the short stack by the microwave. Then he began picking through the liquor bottles crowding the countertop, twirling and tilting them so he could read their labels.

Out of the corner of her eye, something snagged her attention, and she turned her head. The air whooshed from her lungs.

Across the room, Aiden captured her gaze. He stood out, like the lone star in a black night sky. For a moment, the world stopped. The chaos swirling around her receded and he was all that existed.

It'd been so long since she'd allowed herself to even sneak a glance at him that she stared, absorbing him into her heart. The muted lighting picked out strands of russet brown and rich auburn in his dark hair, and carved shadows beneath the sharp angles of his cheekbones.

He was beautiful.

As was Samantha Whitaker by his side.

Kyle appeared before her, his wide shoulders blocking Aiden from her view.

"Try this." He handed her a red Solo cup filled with bright red liquid. "You'll like this better."

She sipped the fruity drink.

"What do you think?"

"It tastes like punch."

"It is punch." A slow smile lifted one corner of his mouth. "With a little bit of vodka."

She'd never tasted vodka before, but it wasn't nearly as disgusting as beer.

Over and around Kyle's broad shoulders, Brynn snuck glimpses in Aiden's direction. She caught only tiny snippets. His dark eyes touching her face. His fierce scowl burning a hole in Kyle's back.

She hadn't asked Aiden why he disliked Kyle, as Rory suggested, because honestly, she didn't care. Whether or not Aiden liked Kyle had no effect on her feelings. She liked Kyle, and that was all that mattered.

She sipped the delicious drink he'd made her.

So what if Kyle didn't run with the same crowd as her step-brothers did? Or that he wasn't as popular as they were? News-flash: neither was she.

Brett Larson, quarterback for the school's football team, stopped to talk to Kyle and she listened in while they discussed the players on the team and their upcoming schedule. They hated the schedule, and the refs from last week's game, and they'd grown tired of their teammates.

She sucked down more swallows of her drink and considered how much more she'd enjoyed listening to Rory and his friends. Her head spun with a dizzying swoop. She peered into her cup. Unbelievably, she'd consumed less than half of the fruity punch.

Someone cranked the volume on the music. Unable to hear Kyle and Brett, her gaze drifted around the room. Unable to resist, she sought out Aiden.

He was watching her.

Another wave of dizziness struck, and she rubbed her fore-head. Did the vodka make her woozy, or was it Aiden's intense regard?

Brett moved on, and Kyle turned to her with a smile. He said something and waited for her reply.

"What?" She touched her ear. "I can't hear you."

He leaned close and spoke with his mouth near her ear. "I said you're really pretty."

Her cheeks warmed. In fact, she was hot all over. Uncomfort-ably hot.

But Kyle leaned closer. He bent his head low.

She froze. Was he going to kiss her? What would it be like? Would she like it? What if she hated it? What if she was wrong and he was only shifting his weight to the other foot?

She wasn't wrong.

His lips brushed hers.

His mouth was surprisingly cold. But his lips were soft, and the kiss wasn't entirely unpleasant.

She let him explore her mouth, curious what would happen next.

Curious if Aiden was still watching.

Scratch that. She didn't care what Aiden thought. This was her moment. Her moment with Kyle. Her first kiss. That she didn't totally hate.

But what did it mean that she was more interested in Aiden's reaction to the kiss than her own?

Kyle pulled up, and she blinked open her eyes. His mouth moved, but she couldn't hear his words.

She shook her head.

He grasped her hand and tugged. The thumping beat of the music pounded inside her skull as he pulled her through the crowd. At the staircase, he started to climb. Her foot caught on one of the stairs, which seemed to be shifting beneath her feet, and she tripped.

With a hand under her arm, Kyle hauled the rest of the way upstairs. On the landing, the piercing sound of the music was dampened by the floorboards. He pulled her toward an open door.

Her steps faltered. She shouldn't go into a darkened bedroom, she knew, but her jumbled thoughts wouldn't line up in order and she couldn't recall exactly why not. Her heartbeat pounded in her ears, and her head began to ache with throbbing pain. The room was dark and quiet, so she moved toward the door.

Light from the hallway guided her. Until the door closed and plunged them into blackness.

"C-can we turn on a light?" Her voice wavered. "Kyle?"

He touched her arm, and she jerked with surprise. Her cup slipped between her fingers and crashed to the floor. Biting wetness soaked through her blue jeans on one thigh.

"Shh." His hand moved to her waist.

In the dark, she stumbled back.

His hand squeezed her breast, pinching the sensitive nipple between his fingers.

A mortified gasp erupted from her.

"That's it," he said, his words garbled. "Feels good, doesn't it, baby?"

"No—" His mouth clamped on hers, and she twisted her head away. "Kyle, wait. I'm serious."

Rough hands groped her body and rammed between her thighs.

"Kyle!" Fear shot up her spine.

"Relax," he slurred. "You'll enjoy it more if you relax."

"You're hurting me." She shoved at his hand. "Kyle, please. Stop."

A stream of light spilled across the room when the bedroom door opened. Relief swamped her, and she scurried toward the shadowy figure standing in the doorway. Thank God someone had found them in.

"Dude, what are doing?" C.J.'s large frame prevented her escape into the hall.

"Brynn's here." Kyle moved behind her. "She's a little scared."

"Why are you scared?" The light behind him, she couldn't see C.J.'s face, but his head tilted to one side. "There's nothing to be afraid of," he said, his voice smooth as butter.

Slimy, oily butter.

Her stomach heaved.

"That's what I told her." An edge of annoyance crept into Kyle's tone. "You should listen to C.J., Brynn."

"We're not going to hurt you." C.J.'s shoes scraped against the hardwood floors, and then shadow blanketed the room when he eased the door shut. "A girl like you, I'll bet you're going to like it."

In the inky darkness, the sound of the door's lock clicking into place screamed through her.

CHAPTER 7

$\mathcal{T}$error froze her a moment. Then she lunged.

Fingers dug into her arms, and her head jerked back when someone yanked her hair. A cry built in her throat, and she drove her knee upward into a groin.

His sharp curse rang out, and she lurched again for the door.

From behind, a large body toppled her, and she hit the ground with a brutal crack of pain. The blow knocked the air from her lungs.

With desperate gulps, she struggled for breath while groping hands bit at her flesh. Disoriented in the dark, she didn't know who assaulted her. That another attacker lurked in the shadows sent tendrils of terror coiling through her.

Frantic, she shoved at his chest and shoulders until her arms shook, then crumpled under his weight. He dropped back down on top of her and pushed a scream from her.

His hand clamped tight over her mouth. "Shut up. Someone will hear you," Kyle said.

She couldn't breathe. The heft of his big body pressed down on her while his large hand obstructed her airways. Panic welled up and she thrashed her head, trying to escape his airtight grip on her nose and mouth. Her hands balled into fists, she punched wildly at his face and shoulders, but her strikes soon weakened.

He raised up, only to slip and collapse heavily on her again. His weight was crushing her, and he was too drunk to realize it.

He was going to kill her.

She heard laughter. Cold, cruel laughter. It rang in her ears and wrung anguish from her heart.

They enjoyed her fear. Whatever she might've believed about what was happening to her, about what they were doing to her, she knew then that her suffering was the reason for it all.

They wouldn't stop until they'd wrested the darkest pain from her.

Tears leaked from the corners of her eyes while vicious hands pinched and grasped her breasts and between her legs. She was helpless to stop them.

Inside, she was screaming.

With a booming crack, the door exploded.

Light flooded the room. A noise erupted, like a growl and a roar at the same time, and then the weight of Kyle's body lifted off her.

She gasped for air. Her chest burning, she rolled to her side and, with deep, painful gulps, hauled oxygen into her starving lungs. Coughs racked her body. She squeezed her eyes shut against the harsh glare of light and the awful, wonderful sound of flesh pounding flesh.

She pushed up onto her hands and knees, but her limbs were impossibly heavy, as though she moved through thick sludge.

The grotesque pounding stopped, and an oddly tuneful whistle floated through the air.

Then footsteps beat a path toward her.

A hand touched her shoulder where her sweater's torn neckline sagged.

Terror shot through her. She recoiled, but her strength gave out. Dropping hard onto her backside, she blinked through the fog clouding her vision.

Golden brown eyes burned away the haze.

Aiden crouched in front of her. "It's okay. You're safe now, *a rún.*"

The trembling started in her hands but soon spread to the rest of her body. Dark eyes held hers, willing her to wholeness when all she wanted to do was fall apart. Her gaze darted around until she'd found the motionless bodies of both Kyle and C.J.

A sob escaped her, and she clasped a hand over her mouth.

Aiden held his hand out to her. "Whaddya say we get you out of here?"

She loved that idea so much, she clutched his outstretched hand and scrambled to her feet. But the floor shifted under her, and her knees buckled.

Aiden caught her under the arm.

The room pitched again, and she leaned heavily against him. "Sorry," she murmured. "I feel weird."

"Weird how?" He wrapped his arm more tightly around her. "How much did you drink?"

She recalled the fruity punch and glanced over at the red slush splattered across the floor. "I didn't finish my drink."

"That's all you've had?"

"And a sip of really bad beer." A wave of nausea hit her. "Am I drunk?"

"You're not drunk."

They turned toward the door, where suddenly Cian loomed. His gaze swept over Kyle and C.J.'s still-unconscious forms, then landed on her.

She tugged her sweater's tattered neckline up over her shoulder.

Vicious fury vibrated off him.

She shrank back.

68

Behind him, Rory bounded up the stairs. As he approached the, his steps slowed. "What the…?"

"Clear the bedrooms."

At Aiden's order, Cian slid past Rory and moved into the hall.

"Get the drinks from the girls."

Rory cursed and dragged a hand through his dark hair. "Are they drugged?"

"I don't know. Just… get them." Aiden's arm tightened around her shoulders. "I'm taking her home."

An earsplitting bang erupted, and Brynn flinched. At the howl of outrage, she craned her neck to see what was happening, but Aiden kept them moving.

Rory hustled down the stairs, but she navigated the steps more slowly on her shaky legs. The second time she stumbled, Aiden tucked her into his side. She sank into his solid strength.

Down below, Rory moved through the crowd, disarming their female classmates with a charming smile long enough to pluck the red plastic cups from their hands.

He'd collected several cups before anyone realized what he was about. Then the protests began.

"Hey."

"That's mine."

"What are you doing?"

Undaunted, Rory continued snatching cups. "Excuse me. Apologies. So sorry, ladies, but we'll need to be replacing your beverages. It's come to our attention that some fecker pissed in the punchbowl."

"*What?*"

"*Ewwww.*"

"Who even does that?"

"Kyle Pierson." Rory enunciated the name clearly, helpfully lifting his voice above the noise in the room. "And that pissant he hangs out with all the time, C.J. something-or-other?"

"C.J. Moore?"

"That's him. C.J. Moore and Kyle Pierson urinated in your drinks, everyone."

"Those bastards."

"What. The. Hell?"

At the bottom of the stairs, Aiden steered Brynn through the crowd, guiding her between and around people and obstacles. Though they moved through the room unnoticed, she felt like a child who'd misbehaved and been caught in the act.

As they passed, Rory crouched before Whitney and peered deeply into her pretty face. "How you doing tonight? You feeling all right?"

Pink touched Whitney's cheeks when she nodded and handed over her cup without an argument.

Aiden held open the door, and Brynn slipped outside ahead of him.

The chill night air seeped through her thin sweater and she realized she'd left her coat behind. But the thought of returning to that bedroom caused her stomach to wrench, so she resolved to carry on without it.

While the fresh air cleared some of the fog from her head, by the time they reached the park, she was shaking so badly her teeth chattered.

Aiden shrugged out of his jacket and draped it around her shoulders. She muttered her thanks as she slid her arms into the sleeves and wrapped the oversized coat, still warm from his body, snug around her.

When they turned onto their street, her steps slowed. He adjusted his pace, and thankfully, didn't ask her any questions.

On the sidewalk outside their home, she stopped.

The house was dark except for the light from the lamp in the living room that Siobhan often left on if she went to bed before the boys had come home.

Emotion squeezed her throat, and she swallowed with difficulty. "Would you mind not telling my dad about... what happened?"

Probing eyes searched her face. "You didn't do anything wrong."

Then why did she feel so ashamed? "I know."

"Those bastards hurt you." In the strain in his voice, she could hear what it cost him to keep his anger in check. "They're the ones who should be ashamed."

She poked the curb with the toe of her sneaker. If she looked at him, she knew she'd cry.

"Don't let them hurt you a second time."

Her gaze flew to his face. "You think they'll... do it again?"

"There's not a chance in hell of that happening." The glacial certainty in his voice did much to thaw the cold terror creeping up her spine. "They'll never get near you again."

She expelled a deep, steadying breath.

"I meant only that, they hurt you once by using their physical strength against you. Don't let them hurt you again now." His tone gentled. "You did nothing wrong. Don't let them steal your faith in yourself."

A tear did leak out then, but before she could wipe it away, he reached up and caught the droplet with the pad of his thumb.

He flicked it away. "Those bastards aren't worth even one of your tears."

The angry redness of his knuckles drew her gaze. In one spot, the skin had cracked open and blood had seeped from the wound.

"You hurt your hand."

"It's nothing." He slipped his hands into the pockets of his blue jeans.

"It's not nothing." She hugged his coat tight to her body. "I'm sorry."

"Are you kidding?" The shadow of a wicked smile touched his mouth. "I've been dying for a reason to kick Kyle Pierson's ass."

Understanding slammed into her. "You knew he was awful, didn't you? That's why you ruined my date with him?"

All traces of humor vanished from his face. "I didn't know he was capable of something like this. If I had, I never would've let him in the same room with you."

Her head fuzzy, she gave it a shake. "I don't understand. Then why did you do it?"

He studied the ground, then stared off into the distance for a moment. "I overheard him and his buddies talking about you and some other girls."

"What did they say?"

Flecks of agony swirled in his eyes. "It was a game to them. How many girls could they sleep with by the end of the year? Virgins were worth extra points."

Cian's favorite curse word escaped her.

"I assumed they intended to have your consent." Hot fury licked each word. "I'm so sorry I misjudged him."

She snuggled more deeply into his jacket. "It's not your fault."

"I never should've let him near you."

She probably should've been annoyed at his highhandedness, but at the moment, she found it comforting. "And I never would've listened to you. Not for long."

One corner of his mouth lifted. "I can be fairly persuasive when I wanna be."

His almost-smile touched her heart. Had she ever seen him smile before?

"I wish you'd told me," she said softly.

"I wish I'd told you, too."

They entered the house through the back door. All was quiet when he walked with her up the stairs. She stepped into her room and flipped on the light.

He stayed in the hallway.

Her chest tightened. "You're leaving, aren't you? You're going back to that party."

"I have to." A grimace pulled down the corners of his mouth. "Are you okay?"

"I'm okay," she lied.

She didn't want him to leave, but she could think of no reason why he should stay. At her sides, she'd clenched her fists tight, and she forced herself to relax them.

He started to turn away.

"Wait."

He turned back.

Her courage deserted her. "I, uh... I.... Do you guys have a family whistle?"

Surprise flickered across his expression. "It's just something we used to do when we were kids."

"Will you teach it to me?"

His smile dissolved. He obviously didn't want her to learn the family whistle.

The reasons why hurt too much to contemplate.

"Never mind. Forget I said anything." She inched the door forward.

He flattened his palm against the wood. "One day, I'll teach it to you. I promise."

Despite all that had happened that evening, a featherlight brush of pleasure tickled her heart.

From her bedroom window, she watched him emerge from around the side of the house and set off in the direction they'd just come.

Even after he'd disappeared into the dark night, she remained at the window, knowing Samantha Whitaker would be waiting for him at the party.

CHAPTER 8

The next morning, Brynn couldn't make herself get out of bed. She remained burrowed beneath the covers well past noon, then ventured out only long enough to pee and grab her book before rushing back to the safety of her warm cocoon.

Monday, she skipped school, complaining of a migraine headache.

Tuesday, she repeated the lie.

Wednesday, when her dad threatened to call the doctor, she crawled from bed to shower and dress for school.

She did get sick then, and twice more before fourth period.

Bile rose in her throat when she entered Mr. Strickland's classroom as the final bell rang. Her pulse throbbed in her ears with a nauseating thud.

Though Kyle wasn't at his desk when she slid into her seat, Brynn was about to dash to the restroom once more when Samantha Whitaker nudged her arm.

A grimace contorted the pretty brunette's fine features when she held out a folded piece of notebook paper.

Warily, Brynn accepted the note and unfurled the edges.

Kyle won't be here. He thought it'd be best if he changed his class schedule around.

Brynn stared down at the untidy handwriting, slowly absorbing the information. Her head snapped up, but Sam's attention remained fixed on Mr. Strickland at the front of the classroom.

Just then, Aiden leaned forward in his seat. Warm brown eyes raked over Brynn .

Her mind raced, trying to piece it all together. With her pencil, she scribbled a reply below his messy script. *You did this?*

She refolded the note and handed it back to Sam, who grudgingly passed it on to Aiden.

Brynn watched him read, then scrawl a response with his left hand.

She snatched the paper from Sam and fumbled to open it.

Yes.

One word.

Brynn pressed the note to her chest.

One word that meant everything.

Sudden tears brimmed in her eyes, and she scratched her reply. *Thank you.*

Sam glared daggers at her when Brynn passed her the note, and again when Aiden returned it.

You're welcome.

A moment later, a grumble of annoyance from Sam announced the arrival of a fresh note.

How pissed do you think we can make her?

Unbelievably, Brynn smiled, though she quickly concealed the wide grin behind her hand. *She's pretty pissed now.*

Indeed.

EVEN AFTER THE leaves had disappeared from the trees and the first winter storm of the year had dumped piles of snow on top of them, memories of what had happened at that party terrorized Brynn nightly.

Cian and Rory didn't invite her to any more parties, which suited Brynn just fine, as did the fact that the mere handful of times she set eyes on either Kyle or C.J., they immediately retreated in the opposite direction.

Indeed, the two had become sudden social outcasts as gossip about the party circulated the hallways at school. To Brynn's utter relief, her involvement in the story had been omitted and all that remained was the disgusting fact that Kyle Pierson and C.J. Moore had peed in the punchbowl.

Still, shame began to take root deep inside her.

Needing a distraction from the ugly, accusing voices in her head, when her dad purchased the Mitchells' rundown old house with a plan to renovate it and resell for a hefty profit, Brynn all but begged him to let her help.

At first, he only asked her to keep track of his expenses on a spreadsheet, as she'd offered to do the night of the party, but as the renovation got underway, his long days grew even longer.

Stress took up permanent residence on his face, around his eyes, and shortened his temper. One evening, when his cell phone rang fourteen times in the span of two hours, he flung the device into the sofa cushions and stalked out of the house.

The next time the phone rang, Brynn answered it, and soon she had taken over answering all of his calls. She organized his messages by order of importance and passed on only the most critical communications right away. Everything else she typed up on a prioritized list that she gave him at the end of each day. A few calls, she even handled herself.

Soon, her dad set her up with a desk and a computer at his office, and Brynn spent a couple of hours there every day after school logging receipts, answering the phone, and keeping her dad's calendar of appointments.

When an emergency at the Mitchell house delayed him from showing a house, Brynn looked up the address and headed over to meet the potential buyers. Her dad had given her the security code, and she was able to let the young couple and their two children inside the house to begin viewing the three-bedroom Cape Cod while they waited for Brynn's dad to arrive.

Brynn talked with them as they moved through the house, discussing what they liked and didn't like about the home and how they'd arrange their furniture if they were to buy it.

On the back deck, she pointed out the massive oak tree at the far end of the property and admitted how much she'd enjoyed climbing trees when she was a kid. They'd laughed, and tossed around the possibility of building their kids a treehouse before returning indoors.

The next day, the couple called to make an offer on the home.

While she helped her dad in the office, Aiden and his brothers worked with her uncle and his crew over at the Mitchell house.

One snowy Saturday in December, she holed up in the mobile trailer her uncle used for an onsite office logging the mound of receipts she'd gathered from the crew. When her shoulders started to ache from hunching over her laptop, she took a short break to refill her water cup and use the restroom.

But when she returned to her desk, a candy bar had appeared on the keyboard.

She glanced around, but she was alone inside the small trailer. Had one of the guys come looking for her and forgotten it? Would they come back for the chocolate bar later?

Her stomach let loose with any angry growl. She couldn't eat it, could she?

For the next hour, the candy bar tormented her. Just when she'd reached the limits of her willpower and made her move for the treat, the door to the trailer burst open and Aiden swept inside on a blast of frigid winter air.

Dark eyes swept over her. As he crossed to her desk, a short stack of receipts in his hand, he studied her face with a heavy, intense focus, as though assessing whether she was about to have a mental breakdown or dissolve into hysterics.

Though she very much wanted to do both, pretty much all the time, she smiled.

He handed her the receipts.

"Hey, is this yours?"

He glanced at the candy bar. "It's for you."

"You don't want it?"

"I bought it for you."

Surprise rippled through her like a mini earthquake. "Why?"

"Because I wanted to."

Then he plunged out into the cold.

Chocolate had never tasted so good.

After that, every time she visited the worksite, she discovered another sweet treat. Usually he chose something chocolate, but every now and then, she'd find an enormous cookie or a glazed doughnut waiting for her.

Once, she considered it was all part of some evil plot he'd hatched to destroy her life by making her fat on top of being unpopular and unloved, but then she eyed the oversized blueberry muffin on the desk and decided she didn't care what his ploy might be.

She sank her teeth into the buttery warmth. Flavor exploded in her mouth, and a throaty moan escaped her, just as he appeared at the door.

A slow smile tilted up the corners of his soft mouth. "That good?"

Heat rushed into her cheeks. Muffin stuck in her throat, and unable to speak, she nodded.

His smile, devoid of conceit or callousness, transformed his handsome face into one of heartbreaking beauty. Without a doubt, his genuine smile was far more delicious than all the sweet treats in the world.

He handed her a pile of receipts.

She swallowed the bite of muffin. "You know, you don't have to be so nice to me. I'm fine."

"I know ye are."

She squirmed beneath his assessing gaze. "How did you get him to transfer classes?"

"I told him the truth."

"What truth?"

"Dat I don't know if he drugged your drink, but if I ever find out dat he did, he's goin' to regret it. If I find out he's tried to talk to ye, he's goin' to regret it." His voice dropped, low and lethal. "And if I find him in the same room wit ye ever again, I'm goin' to kill him."

A shiver skittered up her spine. "That's a little dramatic. Did he believe you?"

"He did." He regarded her with eyes as cold as a Chicago winter. "One ting I will say about Kyle, he is not stupid."

With the extra help from Brynn and her stepbrothers, her dad and uncle completed the Mitchell house renovation two days ahead of schedule.

The day the home went up for sale, they received four offers and, after a short bidding war, they pocketed twice the profit her dad had anticipated gaining in the endeavor.

She hadn't seen her dad so happy in... well, ever.

A week after Christmas, Aiden turned eighteen.

Brynn remembered Siobhan had once mentioned Aiden's favorite meal back home had been a traditional Irish stew, so after a chat with her stepmom, Brynn made the trek to the grocery store and filled her shopping cart with all the items she'd need to make the dish. She picked up potatoes, beef, and an assortment of vegetables, along with a box of birthday candles and the ingredients to make him a chocolate cake.

As she made her way up and down the grocery aisles, she realized she had started to feel a little like herself again. The oppressive weight sitting on her chest these past months had eased, and she'd even started sleeping through the night again. For the first time since the party, she'd started to believe she was going to be okay.

Largely because of Aiden.

Mostly because of Aiden.

Every time she'd tried to turn inward, he'd drawn her out again. With little things, like chocolate and teasing smiles, he'd kept her from completely shutting out the rest of the world.

At night, when the nightmares visited, memories of his solid warmth or the feel of his arms around her was often the only thing that quieted the chaos inside her. In the moment of her greatest peril, he'd made her feel safe.

She owed him so much. She wanted to thank him, though she suspected he'd never acknowledge the significance of what he'd done for her. So she'd settle for making him a birthday dinner.

On the walk home, she paid no mind to the brisk wind that nipped at her cheeks and lifted her face to soak in the bright sunlight.

But when she arrived home, she stumbled to a stop on the sidewalk. One of the grocery bags slipped through her fingers and dropped hard onto her foot.

Pain throbbed in her toes, and she fought back tears as she stared at the big white For Sale sign that'd been staked into the ground in their front yard.

~

AIDEN'S BIRTHDAY dinner went downhill from there.

While Irish stew may have been his favorite, Cian and Rory

loathed the dish and politely refused to touch the stuff. At the same time, her dad and Siobhan chattered nonstop about the two homes they'd viewed earlier in the day and had all but decided to put in an offer on one of them.

The boys' lack of enthusiasm for her cooking didn't carry over to the prospect of moving, despite the fact that it'd be their second move in less than a year. Indeed, they had nothing negative to say about the proposition whatsoever. The traitors.

But the real blow came when she set Aiden's birthday cake loaded down with eighteen fiery candles before him.

Recoiling, he gaped at her as though she'd plopped down a slaughtered kitten. "What's this?"

"It's a birthday cake."

"Right. What's it for?"

"For your birthday."

Shadows flickered across his face as he frowned at the flames. "Ye shouldn't have done that."

"I wanted to." Her stomach knotted. "I thought you'd like it."

"I like it," Cian jumped in.

"Aiden Joseph, what's gotten into you?" Siobhan snapped. "Brynn worked hard to do this for you. Thank yer sister."

At the last, Aiden flinched, but his gaze remained locked on Brynn. "Thank you," he said softly.

She lifted her shoulders. "It's nothing. Really."

Rory pointed his fork and the flaming cake pan. "Why don't ye blow out the candles so we can eat it?"

Aiden appeared slightly ill as he ate a small piece of cake, and the moment the last bite disappeared into his mouth, he fled downstairs.

When they returned to school after the winter break, a new student had taken Kyle's seat in fourth period. He had bright red hair and a goofy smile that instantly put Brynn at ease.

Mr. Strickland introduced him, explaining that he'd relocated to Chicago from Indiana. Brynn experienced a pang of sympathy when she considered how nervous and out of sorts she felt by her family's upcoming move, and she wasn't going to have to change schools.

She offered him a small smile. "Hi, I'm Brynn."

"Harry," he said.

"How do you like Chicago so far?"

"It's cool." His head bobbed. "It's a lot different than Indianapolis."

"Do you miss it?"

"I miss my friends, but our new house is pretty sweet."

At that, some of her own anxiety about moving receded. "What do you think about the school so far?"

"It's all right." His goofy smile made an appearance. "I figure we only have a few more months left before graduation anyway, so how bad can it be?"

Brynn liked Harry, and by mid-February they'd formed an easy rapport.

Over the next several weeks, as her childhood home sold and she prepared for the move to a new house, she tried to emulate Harry's upbeat attitude about his own displacement.

As moving day neared, she spent fewer hours at her dad's office after school to return home and work on boxing up her belongings. On this particular day, Siobhan had gone to a doctor's appointment, and the house was quiet when she let herself in the back door.

Upstairs, her packing was interrupted by the laundry basket overflowing with dirty clothes in the corner of her bedroom. She crammed as much into the basket as she could lift and hauled the heap to the basement, but as she loaded her garments into the washing machine, a soft sound froze her in her tracks.

A giggle.

A girly giggle.

Against her will, her feet carried her toward the source of the sound. Inch by gut-wrenching inch, she approached the door to Aiden's bedroom.

There she stopped. The door slightly ajar, she peered through the crack. His broad back faced her, and she watched undetected.

Brynn didn't know the girl whose waist his hands gripped and whose mouth his lips claimed in a soft, lingering kiss.

With the visceral, gutting pain that slashed through her, she gasped.

He turned his head and golden brown eyes speared her to the spot. Something dangerous and fiery flashed in his dark irises, but she couldn't decipher it's meaning through the shattered lens of her breaking heart.

Letting go of the girl's small waist, Aiden strolled toward Brynn.

His eyes held hers as he eased the door shut.

Echoes of pain ripping through her, Brynn stumbled away. At the washing machine, she shoved the rest of her clothes into the basin and slammed the lid closed. Unable to see past the tears filling her eyes, she cranked the dial and darted for the stairs. But no matter how she tried, she couldn't outrun the truth.

That she loved more than Aiden's smile.

CHAPTER 9

*O*n a dreary day in March, Brynn loaded the boxes that contained her entire life into the back of a moving van and watched it drive away. From the back seat of her dad's car, the only home she'd ever known faded from sight.

She tried to convince herself she didn't care about the house, and that her anxiety didn't seem to be growing right along with Siobhan's swelling belly, but it was no use. With every new change in her life, she only became more lost and alone.

Their new house was larger than the old one, and as long as Rory and Cian continued to share a bedroom once the baby arrived, it had enough bedrooms for Aiden to move out of the basement.

Unfortunately, he moved into the bedroom next to hers. Worse, the two rooms shared a connecting bathroom, and Brynn just knew the first time he brought a girl home she was going to cry. Or vomit.

Probably both.

Lost in her brooding thoughts, she was surprised when Harry appeared at her locker. His face flushed as bright red as his ginger hair, and his tongue tripped over the flurry of words that shot from his mouth. Through the sputters and stammers, it took her a moment to realize he was asking her to go with him to the prom.

Her first instinct was to flatly refuse. She didn't want to go to any more parties, even a school-sponsored one, but it'd obviously cost him a lot to ask her. In truth, she found his awkwardness endearing.

So she accepted his invitation.

She tried to get excited about attending the foremost social event on the school calendar, but she simply couldn't muster any enthusiasm. Since he'd asked her prom, Harry hadn't spoken more than three words to her, and she hated how uncomfortable they now acted around each other.

She also hated shopping. She hated it so much that she waited until the last weekend before the dance to go to mall to buy a dress.

At breakfast Saturday morning, she caught her dad before he left for work. "Can I borrow your credit card? I have to buy a dress for the prom."

Her dad retrieved his wallet from the hip pocket of his work slacks. Sliding the card from its slot, he held it out to her. "Maybe your mother would like to go with you."

Brynn and Siobhan blinked at one another.

"What's this?" Siobhan asked.

"The senior prom?" Brynn took the thin plastic card from her dad. "It's a dance at school. It's kind of a big deal here."

"It sounds lovely."

Brynn's dad refilled his coffee cup. "As I understand it, shopping for the dress is a pretty big deal, too."

Siobhan blinked, then understanding struck. "Oh. Sure. Of course." She pushed to her feet, a difficult feat with her ginormous belly. "That sounds like fun. Let me change my clothes, and I'll come with you."

On occasion, Brynn had overheard the other girls at school

talk about shopping with their moms, and she couldn't stem the fountain of hope that bubbled up at the chance of experiencing what every other teenage girl did—an afternoon of shopping, and bonding, with a mother.

Maybe not *her* mother, but still.

Reality, however, was a little different than Brynn had pictured it in her mind. Probably because Siobhan had three boys and was eight months pregnant, and Brynn had only ever shopped with her dad, a man who considered the task loathsome and, when forced to do it, attempted to complete the job in as short a timeframe as possible, often giving Brynn mere minutes to make her selections before heading to the store's exit.

Whatever the reason, both women struggled with the moment.

Brynn visited three stores before she found a dress she liked well enough to try on, but when she emerged from the dressing room, Siobhan was nowhere in sight. Brynn returned the dress to the rack and continued on to the next store. As she passed by the food court, she spotted Siobhan in line at the pizzeria, and it was right about that time that Brynn realized the mother-daughter thing just wasn't going to happen for them.

The night of the dance, Brynn added some curls to her long hair and stepped into the plum cocktail dress she'd picked out while Siobhan ate pizza.

Minutes before Harry would arrive to pick her up, she headed downstairs.

But as she descended the bottom stairs, Aiden approached. Passing by on his way to the kitchen, his steps slowed when he spotted her. He stopped before her.

She eyed him with warily. "You're not going to… do anything, are you?"

Sorrow touched his features. "I am not."

The leaden pit that formed in her stomach whenever she recalled Kyle or C.J. or what happened at that party made a sudden, sickening appearance. "Is there anything I should know about Harry?"

"He hasn't given me any reason to warn you off him." The gold in his eyes glittered. "Yet."

She exhaled a breath she hadn't realized she'd been holding.

Then she took in his blue jeans and T-shirt. "Aren't you going?"

"The girl I wanted to take is unavailable."

The stab of jealousy barely hurt anymore. Too much scar tissue had built up over the wounds for her to feel the fresh jabs.

In the living room, Cian, Rory, and her dad watched the baseball game playing on the TV while Siobhan knitted something yellow and fuzzy. Brynn claimed a seat on the sofa to wait for Harry, who was a few minutes late by that point.

She fussed with her flowy skirt, smoothing the delicate fabric flat to prevent wrinkles, and turned her attention to the game. Carrying a glass of milk, Aiden returned from the kitchen and settled at the opposite end of the sofa.

After one inning and roughly twenty minutes of waiting, a stomach-turning dread began to crawl up her spine. She slipped her cell phone from the small clutch she'd bought that matched her dress, but she hadn't missed any calls or texts from Harry. She brushed aside her worry and readjusted her skirts.

When the next inning ended, Rory climbed to his feet. At the front door, he lifted his jacket off the coat hook.

Siobhan smoothed a hand over her large belly. "And where do you think you're going?"

"To meet up with some friends."

As underclassmen, Cian and Rory wouldn't be able to attend the senior prom unless they went with a senior, but that night, Brynn knew of several parties taking place that her stepbrothers would surely have been invited to.

"Wait until Brynn's date gets here," Siobhan said. "We want to take some pictures with all of you."

Brynn wanted to argue as Rory flopped into an armchair, but her throat had tightened, and she didn't trust she'd be able to speak. She pretended immense interest in the activity taking place on the television.

Excruciating seconds ticked by until another half an hour had passed. Both Cian and Rory typed away on their phones, likely sending texts to their friends to explain that they were running late, and why.

Why hadn't Harry done the same?

She stared hard at the TV.

Had something happened to him? Was he sick? Involved in an accident?

Or was it just her?

As the minutes continued to slip away, old memories began to rise from the shadows of her mind. She recalled the expressions on the teachers' faces as they'd huddled together, speaking in hushed voices while Brynn had waited for her mom to pick her up at the school. All the other kids had gone home and only Brynn remained. When darkness began to fall, she remembered how their looks had changed from annoyance to concern, then to pity.

With a mental shake, she shook off the past. The past had nothing to do with today.

Except for the waiting.

And the wondering if something awful had happened.

And the wishing someone would tell her what the heck was going on.

And the worrying that the truth would hurt more than the waiting and not knowing ever could.

Across from her, her dad's knee bounced like the shaft of a jackhammer.

If Harry had been delayed, why hadn't he called? She sent him a text asking where he was, and then another less than five minutes later to inquire if he'd changed his mind about going to the dance. Five minutes after that, she even told him it was fine if he had changed his mind, but to please let her know so she wouldn't worry.

But it wasn't fine, and she'd begun to suspect that, for the rest of her life, she'd wonder and worry if it was her. If she simply wasn't enough.

No response from Harry came to her phone.

Nearly two hours after the time he told her he'd pick her up, she stopped obsessively checking her phone. She stopped fussing with her skirts, knowing it no longer mattered if they became wrinkled.

Her dad, who'd been pacing back and forth in front of the window, ceased.

Discreetly, Siobhan signaled the boys that they could leave and Rory and Cian slipped silently from the room. But Aiden hesitated.

She hated him all the more for it.

With an odd sort of detachment, she considered that the threat of tears didn't loom over her. Maybe she was numb. Maybe she no longer experienced shock at what all seemed so predictable. Inevitable.

Even so, she didn't trust herself to speak. Silently, she stood and forced herself to walk, not run, to the stairs. She kept her spine straight and her shoulders squared when she slunk from the room.

In her bedroom, she locked the door behind her.

Almost immediately, a knock sounded.

She ignored it and sank down on the edge of her bed. It was probably her dad, but there was nothing he could say that'd make the situation suck any less. Why pretend there was?

After a prolonged wait, footsteps retreated down the hall.

Leaning forward, she propped her elbows on her knees and rubbed the ache between her eyebrows. The tears did come then.

The bathroom door swung open. Her head came up to find Aiden standing in her bedroom.

She glared, determined not to let him see her tears. "Go away."

Of course, it was too late to hide the wet streaks on her face, so she lifted her chin, determined instead not to let him know it bothered her that he'd already seen her tears.

His expression gave little away. "I'm starting to think you were right."

"Right about what?"

"There's no such thing as The One." His mask of indifference suffered a crack. "At least, not for me."

Her soft chuckle held no humor. "I guess you'll have to stay single forever, then. Not to worry. I suspect any woman who agreed to marry you would also have murdered you in your sleep."

"Would you look at that?" A crooked smile pulled up the corner of his mouth. "I knew there was a smartass buried somewhere deep inside you."

"Why are you here?" she snapped.

"Because you need me."

A sneer curled her lip. "I do *not* need you."

"You do." Sudden emotion churned in his dark eyes. "You need me to tell you the truth."

Her stomach dropped to the floor. Moments ticked by while dread at what he would say next congealed in the pit of her stomach.

"The truth about what?" she asked, though she desperately didn't want to know.

"All this time I've been looking for The One, I knew I'd never find her."

Resentment burned in her chest to be reminded of his manwhoring, especially now. "Oh, yeah? Well, you certainly gave it your all."

"I'll never find her, because she doesn't exist. Like ye said."

Something in his tone riddled her with doubts, but she shook them off. "You wouldn't think it'd be so hard, finding the perfect big boob, tiny brain combo."

"I told ye, it's not about her looks."

"Then what?" Weariness snapped the last of her patience. "What in the hell are you looking for?"

"The one who can make me forget."

"Forget what?"

His Adam's apple bobbed. "You."

Her brain stuttered.

When he bent his head and drove his hand through his dark hair, she saw that it trembled.

Dazedly, she gaped at him. "I don't understand what you're saying."

He lifted his gaze, and she gasped. More heartache than she'd experienced in a thousand lifetimes swirled in his eyes. He showed it all to her, without holding back even one teardrop of his anguish.

Wild flutters tickled her belly. "But you hate me."

He gave his head a slow shake.

"Yes, you do." Her voice rose with her indignation.

"I do not hate you." Heat seared each word. "I hate that our parents are married and now you're my sister. I hate that I cannot be with you. I hate that no matter how many other girls I try to sleep with, none of them can make me forget you. Forget how much I want you. How much I need—" He bit out a curse.

She shot to her feet. "What? What do you need?"

"It doesn't matter."

"It matters to me." Because though she couldn't begin to guess what he might say, she knew without a doubt that she needed it, too.

He stared at the floor at her feet while her heart tried to thrash its way out of her body.

"All my life, I never asked for anything. I never wanted more than I'd already been given." Softness and steel fused in his voice. "All the bullshit with my dad, and the way people looked at us because we were bastards, I didn't fight it. I didn't demand they treat us better. I knew who and what I was, and I didn't give a shit what anyone else thought about anything. I was happy. I was content. I didn't need a goddamn thing from this world." His eyes captured hers. "Until I met you."

Her throat parched, she swallowed with difficulty. "People were mean to you?"

He rolled his shoulders. "They looked down on us."

"Why? Because you don't know who your dad is?"

"You're kind of missing the point of everything else I said."

"I heard you. I'm"—she made a motion with her hand —"processing."

"Take your time." He leaned with one shoulder against the doorjamb and folded his arms, the picture of relaxed patience.

She searched his face for signs of deception, but found only a tender vulnerability that speared her heart. Dare she believe he was telling her the truth?

"Why?"

A pucker appeared over one of his eyebrows. "Why didn't I tell you?"

"Why me?"

The shadows cleared. "You're kind, and sweet, fiercely so, and the way you look at me—"

Furious heat rushed into her cheeks. She was so obvious, he'd known all along how she felt about him.

Bare feet appeared in her line of sight. Then he slipped a hand beneath her chin and gently lifted. "Don't hide it from me. Please. I need it. You're the only one who's ever looked at me like that."

Like a lovesick fool? "Girls at school look at you like that every day."

"It's not the same."

She rolled her eyes.

He dragged the pad of his thumb across her cheekbone. "It's not the same because they're not you."

Her breaths came short and shallow. She'd never been so close to him. To the chaos in his eyes.

"You look deeper. You see me. The real me." He bent his head until his forehead touched hers. "And you like what you see. Like you think I matter. No one's ever looked at me like that before."

She wanted to deny every last bit of what he said, but his scent teased her senses and claimed her awareness. She closed her eyes and inhaled.

Her eyes flew open. "What do you mean, the girls you *try* to sleep with? You meant all the girls you *do* sleep with, right?"

"I said what I meant." He eased back one step, and another.

"Look, I'm a virgin, okay? I need you to explain to me."

"I haven't been able to, uh… rise to the occasion." His shoulders lifted when he drove both hands into the front pockets of his blue jeans. "I can't… do it. Not with any of them. Believe me, I tried."

Her eyes went wide. "Maybe you should talk to a doctor."

He dropped his chin and pierced her with a pointed look. "There's nothing physically wrong with me."

"How do you know? I mean, if you can't—"

Exasperation and amusement battled for dominance of his features. "Trust me, I know. Let's just say I've independently verified my, uh, prowess."

"Oh." Understanding struck. "Oh!"

Why did the thought of him bringing about his own pleasure make her skin flush so hot?

"But even in that, only you—thoughts of you—will bring the thing about."

He thought about her when he masturbated? "This is a joke, right?"

He glanced down. "What do you think?"

Proof of his arousal pressed against the fly of his blue jeans.

Shock ricocheted through her body with a dizzying rush that left her shaking all over. "What does this mean?"

A heavy, irrefutable grief settled on his shoulders. "Nothing. It doesn't mean anything. Because our parents are married."

"Then why did you tell me all this?" The plaintive wail burst from her.

"Because you're incredible, and if fuckwits at school cannot see it, then fuck them."

Misery and anger and self-doubt were a volatile mix inside her. Finally, she blew. "Prove it."

"Excuse me?"

"I don't believe you. I think you're lying."

"Why would I lie about this?"

"To hurt me. To embarrass me. To make me believe you want me just so you can break my heart again."

His features contorted. "That's demented, and it's not what I'm doing. And when did I break your heart?"

"Every day. Every stupid day, with every stupid girl you kiss." Her voice broke with her sob. "If you want me, then show me. Prove I'm not wrong for wanting to believe you."

He went unnaturally still. "Ye know I cannot do that."

She rushed forward.

His eyes flared with a warning, and she tripped to a stop.

How had she not seen it before? It'd been there all along. Not disdain or loathing, but alarm. Fear.

Panic, imploring her to stay back.

She didn't heed his warning.

He remained motionless when she placed her hands on his chest, rose up on her tiptoes, and brushed her lips against his.

The thrill that whipped through her pulled a soft moan from the back of her throat, which tore a growl from somewhere deep inside Aiden's chest. His arms closed around her, strong and gentle, possessive but tender, while his mouth nibbled hers in a soft, claiming kiss that set her world spinning wildly around her.

She was kissing Aiden, and he was kissing her back.

Though she should stop the kiss, she didn't. Though she should resist her stepbrother, she couldn't. Instead, she reveled in him. She relished his spicy scent and soothing heat. She gloried in the luscious taste and feel of him. In the proof of his desire pressing against her stomach.

Helpless to stop herself, she plunged headlong into him. Her heart galloping, she became lost in his kiss. With soft bites and small licks, his mouth cherished her. It was everything she'd ever wanted.

No matter that it could tear her family apart.

Then it was over, and he was turning away.

When he reached the doorway to their shared bathroom, the heat his kisses stoked inside her flamed out, like a bucket of ice water splashed over a fire.

"Wait, you're leaving? After everything you just said? After that kiss? You're just going to leave me feeling all... all...?"

What was she feeling? She'd never felt this way before, but she liked it. She liked it a lot.

She wanted more.

She *needed* more.

"I never should've come." Raw emotion frayed the edges of his voice. "I only wanted you to know the truth."

"Aiden, wait." She touched his arm. "Stay. Please. Show me what happens next."

His face leached of color. "Our parents are downstairs."

"We'll be quiet."

"Jesus—"

A frantic, irrational fear gripped her. "You were right. I—I need you."

"I cannot stay," he croaked.

"You can't leave." Her hold on his arm tightened. "You—you —you can't say all those things to me and then—then... leave me."

In his eyes and on his face, a kaleidoscope of regret and longing played out.

"You and me, it can never happen." He brushed her cheek with the back of his hand. "I'm sorry."

Mortification swamped her.

All the hurts in her heart seemed to flood forth at once. Harry and Kyle, her mom, and now Aiden. They all mixed and churned inside her. Too many rejections. Too much pain for one fragile heart.

"What is wrong with me?" she whispered. "Why can't anyone love me?"

Tender grief twisted his features. "Nothing is wrong with you. You're perfect." He pushed a lock of her hair off her forehead, then dropped his hand away. "Perfect in every way. Except one."

Her heart shattered. "What? Please tell me what it is."

"You're my sister."

CHAPTER 10

*F*our days later, Siobhan gave birth to a baby girl.

Brigid Jane Hathaway was wrinkly and screechy, and when Brynn cradled the baby's tiny, wriggling body in her arms, she decided little Brigid was the sweetest thing she'd ever seen.

Siobhan picked the baby's name to match that of the Celtic goddess of poetry, and her noble brood now included a saint, a warrior, a king, and a poet.

Brynn was still just a hill.

The first night, her dad stayed at the hospital with Siobhan and the baby, but he came home briefly the next day to grab a shower and a change of clothes before heading back. She didn't talk to him again until the following evening when he called to check in.

"How's everything there?" he asked. "You doing okay?"

"Everything's fine. How's Brigid?"

"Ah, she's amazing." Her dad's wonder-filled voice crackled through the phone's crappy speaker. "I can't wait to bring her home. Should be sometime tomorrow or the next day."

"You're not coming home tonight?"

"Siobhan and the baby need more time to recover. The nurse promised me she'll spring us the minute she's able. What about you? Any Saturday night plans?"

Shock stole Brynn's voice.

Did she have any plans? She hadn't set eyes on Aiden since he'd kissed her and told her she was The One. The boys were out, and Molly, who had planned to come over and spend the night with Brynn, had contracted the stomach flu, which meant Brynn had the entire house to herself.

Oh, and it was her birthday.

She mumbled some non-answer that satisfied her dad, then disconnected the call.

Standing in the kitchen, she gaped at the cell phone cradled in her palm, too stunned to move.

It'd probably just slipped his mind. She couldn't fault him for forgetting. With so much going on the last few days, it was completely understandable.

Any minute now, he'd remember the date and call her right back to wish her a happy birthday.

She stared at her phone, waiting.

But the phone didn't ring.

Brynn abandoned the device on the kitchen counter.

It was fine. Really, it was. So he forgot. So what? That didn't mean he didn't care about her. Of course he did. Siobhan and the baby needed him. They were his family now.

And Brynn? Well, she was eighteen. Technically an adult, even if she didn't feel like one.

Even if she felt like a little girl who missed her dad.

A vise clamped tight around her chest. How could her own father have forgotten her birthday?

When the boys left without saying anything, she'd been disappointed, but the sting hadn't lasted long. The fact was, they hadn't spent the previous seventeen years celebrating this day with her.

With a mental shake, she pushed away from the counter. It

was her birthday, dammit. If no else cared, she'd have to throw herself a party.

In the pantry, she flipped on the light. Stretching up on her tiptoes, she pulled a brownie mix down off the top shelf and, at the island, dumped the ingredients into a large mixing bowl. She started the oven warming, then set to work stirring the contents of the bowl.

With every little twinge of disappointment that struck her, she whipped the mixture more vigorously. They had a special bond, she and her dad. Nothing could sever their connection. Not her mom leaving them. Not him remarrying and starting a new family. Through it all, they'd remained close and they would do so now as well. She'd make sure of it.

When her arm ached from beating brownie batter, she poured the concoction into a pan and set it in the warm oven to bake. Then she gathered the butter, cocoa, and powdered sugar and carried them to the counter. While she whisked together the ingredients, she pondered all the ways she could cement her relationship with her dad.

What if she picked up some extra hours at his office? That way, he'd be able to spend more time with Siobhan and the baby, at least at first. But also, she would get to spend more time with him, and by helping out, she'd have a chance to prove to him how valuable she was to have around.

She'd help him make more money, too, which would make Siobhan happy.

If she did all that, he'd have to love her.

Her mood lifted until she felt as light and fluffy as the chocolate frosting. She set the frosting in the refrigerator to chill while the brownies finished baking, then, though there was no one else home to help her eat it, she ordered a large pizza to be delivered from her favorite restaurant.

It was her birthday, after all.

While she waited for the pizza to arrive, she flipped on the TV in the living room and switched through the channels before landing on a movie she never would've watched if her stepbrothers had been at home. It was a Cinderella retelling that somewhat mirrored her own life—if one of the mean stepsisters was her stepbrother instead. Who also happened to be a prince. Plus, was a thousand times grumpier.

The thought of Aiden as a prince teased a smile to her lips when she paused the movie long enough to remove the brownies from the oven and set them on the cooktop to cool.

Aiden was far from princely. Or saintly, for that matter. But he'd told her she was The One, and she'd never felt more like one of the princesses from the bedtime stories her mom used to read to her.

Brynn's heart swelled to recall his words. To remember the soft, tortured light shimmering in his dark eyes when he'd confessed the truth.

It was the truth, wasn't it? He wouldn't lie about something like that.

Would he?

Doubt kicked in her chest. What if he'd lied only to get her to stop crying? To forget for the moment that Harry had stood her up?

The doorbell's chime jerked her from her thoughts. She paid the delivery guy from the pile of bills her dad had left on the kitchen counter. Balancing the warm, aromatic pizza box in one hand, she snagged the short stack of envelopes from the mailbox before kicking the front door closed with one foot.

She deposited the pizza box onto the coffee table and quickly rifled through the mail. When she flicked to the third correspondence, her hand stilled. Addressed to Aiden, it'd originated from Trinity College in Dublin.

Ireland.

Her stomach clenched. Had Aiden applied to attend the school? Was he leaving?

Brynn choked down a couple of slices of pizza, a task made difficult with her heart wedged in her throat. Though she watched the movie playing out on the television screen, her mind fixated on that letter. What did it say? She could think of only two topics that might be contained within it. Either he'd been accepted for or denied admission to the university.

Her fragile good mood shattered like broken glass.

If Aiden left, would she ever see him again? Would he come home only for special occasions and the few holidays he could manage the long trip overseas? How could she bear seeing him so infrequently? How could he tell her she was The One, and then abandon her?

Panic crawled up her spine, and she surged to her feet. She snagged the pizza box off the coffee table and carried it into the kitchen, where she crammed it inside the refrigerator. She didn't even bother labeling the box with the permanent marker she'd been using to claim her food before the boys ate it.

In the pantry once more, she rummaged around until she found a half-used pack of birthday candles. Only seven remained in the box, well shy of her eighteen years, but she smeared frosting over the brownies and pushed all seven wax sticks into her impromptu birthday cake.

She dug around in the junk drawer and eventually located a lighter. After a few quick strikes to test the flame, she returned to the pan of brownies. But when she bent over the pan, a noise at the back door straightened her spine.

Twisting around, she shoved the lighter into the front pocket of her sweatshirt as Aiden stepped through the archway.

Wild butterfly wings banged to life inside her stomach. "Hey."

His gooey warm gaze dragged down her body with all the delicious promise of the pan of brownies behind her. "Hey."

In the strained silence, the sound of her ragged breathing echoed in her ears. Little erratic whorls that mimicked her heart's chaotic beating. Frantically, she searched her mind for some meaningless words to deflect from her overpowering reaction to him.

But all she could think to do was ask him how his night had gone, except she didn't want to know what he'd been doing or with whom he'd been doing it, so she stayed quiet. Just in case.

She waited for him to sulk off to his bedroom upstairs.

"What's that?" He pointed at the island behind her.

"Uh… nothing." She slanted her body to hide the pan.

"It smells like cake."

"Brownies."

He moved toward her. "Did you make them?"

She slid between him and the island. "They're hot."

He pulled to a stop.

"Too hot to eat." She wrenched around. Using her body to block his view of the pan, she plucked candles from the frosting.

Snatching the last wax stick, she clenched her fists and shoved her hands deep into her sweatshirt's pocket.

With a smile, she faced him. "Would you like one once they're cool?"

He made a quiet study of her. Then the soles of his shoes scuffed against the hardwood floor, and he closed the small space between them. She sucked in a soft breath as the sweet spiciness of his scent teased her nostrils. He reached out.

His large, warm hands stole into either side of her sweatshirt's front pocket. When he pried open her clamped fists, his fingers brushed the sensitive skin of her palms.

He swiped the candles from her grasp and withdrew his hands from her shirt. Head bent, he considered the candles, still dappled with chocolate frosting. Then his gaze swept over to the brownies and their mottled surface.

Dark eyes found hers. "Is it your birthday?"

Her mouth opened and closed while she fumbled for the lie that'd explain away the truth.

Stumped, she shrugged. "Yeah."

"Where's your dad?"

"At the hospital."

He glanced down at the candles, then back up. "He's probably got something great planned for when he gets home."

She jumped on the falsehood. "Yeah, of course he does. He's my dad." A sound like a scoff vibrated in the back of her throat. "He wouldn't forget my birthday."

An odd expression touched his features. Then he gently pushed her aside and slid a candle into the soft brownies.

"Oh, you don't have to—"

He silenced her with a look. When he'd finished positioning each of the candles, he glanced back at her and held out his hand.

She hesitated.

He dropped his chin and his brows knitted together in a stern frown.

She sighed and coughed up the lighter.

Candles aglow, he turned to her.

"I'm not much of a singer." In the dim lighting, the gold in his eyes shimmered like liquid fire. "Make a wish."

Her heart ached from the flood of emotion that rushed in to fill the battered shell. It took her several puffs of air to extinguish the little dancing flames.

"Happy birthday," he said softly. "I'm sorry no one else is here."

She waved her hand, scattering a puff of smoke that had nothing to do with the tears brimming in her eyes. In truth, it no longer bothered her everyone forgot her birthday. In the few minutes since Aiden had appeared, it'd become her most favorite birthday ever.

"I got to eat a whole pizza by myself," she said with a laugh.

He laid his hand over his heart. "You had pizza without me?"

"There might be a piece or two left in the fridge."

While he disappeared behind the refrigerator door, she pulled candles from the brownies. "You received a letter in the mail today."

The refrigerator door shut with a soft thump.

"You been reading my mail?" Beneath the humorous tease in his tone lay a ridge of unease.

She padded into the living room and filched the letter from the coffee table. When she returned, she held the envelope out to him.

He regarded it with suspicion, as though she attempted to pass off a nuclear warhead.

"You applied, didn't you?"

"I doubt they've accepted me."

She waggled the piece of mail. "Why don't you open it and find out?"

He took the letter but dropped it on the counter while he filched a slice of pizza from the box. Half the slice had disappeared inside his mouth before he set it down. He lifted a napkin from the holder and wiped his hands.

Finally, he reached for the envelope.

The tear of paper ripped through the quiet in the house. He extracted the letter and spread out the single tri-folded sheet. The shadow of his long lashes swept down, and he read.

He read maybe four words, then refolded the letter and replaced it inside the envelope. Tossing them onto the counter, he picked up his pizza and tore off another bite with his teeth.

While he chewed, she pondered the changes in his expression and the little lines that formed around his eyes mouth.

"Congratulations," she said.

He used the pad of his thumb to wipe his bottom lip. "I haven't decided if I'm going."

"Why wouldn't you?"

A weighty shadow flickered across his face. "I'm not sure I want to go back."

She hated that shadow. "It's your home."

"They called me a bastard." Though he forced air beneath the words, he couldn't lift their gravity.

"Well, you can be kind of a jerk sometimes."

One corner of his mouth quirked, but in his eyes, the darkness still lurked.

"Was it because your parents weren't married? Because if that's the case, then, like, half the kids at school are bastards." A thought struck. "Wait, am I a bastard, too?"

Gold flecks danced in his eyes. "Ye sound rather pleased by the prospect."

She pulled her bottom lip between her teeth to hide her smile, then gave up the fight. "I don't know. It's sort of badass."

His bark of laughter kicked inside her chest. Warmth prickled across her skin, the same warmth that always prickled across her skin whenever he was nearby, except this time it seeped inside her. Into her bones.

The pleasant sound faded all too quickly.

"You miss it, don't you?" she said.

She'd been so overwhelmed by the sudden, sweeping changes in her life, she'd never given much thought to what it must've been like for Aiden and his brothers, moving to the other side of the world and starting a new school, on top of all the rest of it.

"I do."

"Even though…?" She swallowed the ugly words.

"Most of 'em looked down on us?" He hitched one shoulder. "Like you said, it's my home. Always will be, I suppose."

With the tip of her finger, she traced the thin dark veining on the quartz countertop. "No one looks down on you here."

After a beat, he spoke softly. "I'm glad for it."

She snuck a glance at him from beneath her lashes. Their gazes collided.

Her heart jumped, and a swirl of soft heat sloped through her, filling all the empty places inside her.

"Do you want to know what I wished for?" The question burst from her.

Alarm stole across his features, but he quickly concealed it. "If you tell me, it won't come true."

"I didn't know you were superstitious."

"There's a lot you don't know about me."

With a pang, she realized he was right. Whether he left next month after they graduated or waited until the fall, the window on their time together would soon close. Possibly forever.

She slanted forward and propped her elbows on the countertop. "Quick, tell me something I don't know."

He leaned back, perching his hips against the counter behind him. "I hate strawberries."

"Strawberries?"

"They make me itchy." He raked his fingernails along the side of his neck.

"What else?" she asked, fascinated.

"I think marshmallows are disgusting."

She gasped. "Omigod, you're a monster."

His smile was fleeting. "I hate—" Abruptly, he stopped, and his head dropped when his gaze fell to the floor.

"What?" she whispered. "What do you hate?"

When he looked up, defiance warred with pain on his face. "My dad. I don't even know him, and I fucking hate him."

Then and there, she decided she hated her stepbrothers' biological father, too. She hated anyone or anything that caused that look of anguish in Aiden's dark eyes.

Straightening, she retrieved a knife from the drawer at her hip.

"Is there anything you do like?" She sliced into the brownies.

"Cake," he said as she scooped a large wedge onto a plate and slid the still-warm treat across to him.

A thrill chased through her at the light brush of his fingers against her skin when he accepted the fork that she held out to him.

"You."

Her soft gasp slipped out.

"I like you," he said, each word containing an unbearable tenderness.

Sudden tears closed the back of her throat.

"That makes you sad?"

She gave her head a small shake. "I'm not sad."

"Then why are you crying?"

With a small shrug, she blinked back tears. "Like half an hour ago, I was certain I'd go the rest of my life without anyone every saying that to me."

"Well, then, for the rest of your life, never forget it. I will always like you."

The smile in her heart displayed on her face. "I will always like you, too."

Rather than eat, he studied her face, as though he were cataloguing every detail, even the tiny, insignificant ones.

Her chest constricted. Why did he have to leave? Why had it taken her so long to realize just how much she wanted him to stay?

"I don't want you to go." Grief stole the power from her voice.

His dark eyes glimmered in the soft lighting. "I won't be gone forever."

"When will you come back?"

"Holidays. Summer break. Your birthday." The smile tugged at his reluctant lips. "Next year, I'll come back for your birthday."

Her heart cracked open.

"I wished for you." The confession flew from her. Unease settled on his shoulders, but she plunged ahead. "Th-that we could… k-kiss. Just once. Before you leave."

A storm cloud whipped across his features, but he clenched

his jaw tight, clamping down on the turmoil. "Your dad would not approve."

Panic gripped Brynn. Her feelings for Aiden had changed so suddenly, so completely, she hadn't yet considered what her dad would think about a relationship between them. What would he say if he knew about the chaotic jumble of emotions she was all of sudden feeling for her older stepbrother? What would he say if he knew she'd just asked Aiden to kiss her?

Okay, he wouldn't like it. Though she suspected he wouldn't like her kissing any boys. But one of her stepbrothers?

Would he be mad? Disappointed?

In truth, she didn't know. She'd worked so hard to please him that she no longer knew what she could do to upset him.

But Aiden was probably right. Her dad wouldn't approve.

How far would his disapproval go? Would he yell at her? Ground her? Wish to stop being her dad?

The memory blindsided her. It'd happened not long after her mom had left them, and Brynn had broken down in tears again trying to understand.

"But w-where is she?" Watery hiccups had racked her body. "Why won't she come home?"

"I don't know, honey," her dad had said. "I guess, she didn't want to be a mom anymore."

The old pain slashed a fresh wound. She pushed away the memories.

Aiden watched her, and she could see that he knew she knew he was right. The expression on his beautiful face mirrored the anguish in her heart.

She didn't want him to be right. She didn't want her dad to be angry or disappointed with her, but neither did she want circumstances to keep her and Aiden apart. Not if they wanted to be together. It wasn't fair.

Aiden's words from the other night echoed through her mind. Like him, Brynn had never asked for anything. All the hurt and sorrow and ridicule she'd faced for having lost her mom the way she did, she'd accepted it all without complaint.

Just this once, she wanted something for herself.

More than anything, she wanted Aiden.

She lifted her gaze to his. "My dad isn't here."

"He's earned my respect," he said, a hint of desperation creeping into his tone. "I do not want to betray his trust."

She flinched. "You're not betraying him. We aren't—we wouldn't be doing anything wrong."

"I don't believe he'd see it that way." At the base of his throat, just above the collar of his T-shirt, his pulse throbbed. "He's protective of you."

"He wants me to be happy," she argued.

"So do I."

His clipped reply struck at her heart, but she steeled herself against the pang. "Being with you would make me happy."

The words hung in the air between them. Though he'd managed to banish the tempest from his expression, the storm raged in his eyes.

"No one has to know," she whispered. "It could be our secret."

He exhaled a sharp breath, as though she'd wounded him somehow. "I cannot."

The rejection punctured a hole in the center of her chest, and she ducked her chin to hide her face.

"But…"

Her head came up.

"I cannot… not." Emotion shredded his voice. "I've tried everything. I've fought it—fought you—but nothing ever changes. Nothing makes me want you less."

A dizzying thrill swooped through her, and she gripped the edge of the countertop behind her.

With painful slowness, he moved toward her, as if some force pulled him to her against his will. "The more I resist, the more I want you. No matter what I do, it's only you. Always, you."

Only a whisper of space separated them, but he didn't move to close it.

Uncertain, she searched his expression. "A-are you sure? If you're embarrassed or ashamed—"

In a flash of movement, his warm hands cupped her face. "You think I'm ashamed? Of you?" A nasty curse ripped from him. "I've never wanted anything the way I want you."

She devoured him with her eyes, savoring every morsel of his beauty—his square angle of his jaw, the straight line of his nose, the smooth ridge of his high cheekbones. The swirl of warm gold and delicious brown in his eyes.

"Promise me." The soft rush of his breath teased across her cheek. "No one can find out, not because I'm ashamed of us, but because I couldn't bear it if they separated us."

Inside her, a torrent of emotions let loose. Hope tangled with fear. Hunger with worry. The memory of his taste on her lips exploded in her mind. Pleasure battled with shame.

Desire conquered them all.

"I promise, Aiden." She touched the tips of her fingers to his full bottom lip. "No one will find out."

CHAPTER 11

*T*hen he kissed her.

His mouth brushed hers, and the light contact set off a storm inside her. Butterflies lurched and plunged in her stomach while he took soft tastes of her lips and little nibbles at the corners of her mouth.

When his tongue peeked out for a tiny lick, the floor beneath her feet fractured and crumbled, and she tumbled down, down into the deep, mysterious cavern that was Aiden.

Her world narrowed to contain only him. His warm strength, his incredible scent, the soft brush of his fingers on the side of her face. She clutched fistfuls of his T-shirt, wanting to crawl inside his heart and never leave.

He laced his fingers through her and gently coaxed her toward the stairs. She floated along beside him, her heart soaring and her lips still tingling from his kiss.

At her bedroom, she slipped into the room ahead of him and switched on the lamp on her dresser. He closed the door behind him, but when he clicked the lock into place, a punch of nervous dread struck her.

His head tipped to one side. "What is it?"

Her mouth had gone suddenly dry. Until five seconds ago, she'd only ever kissed one other boy, and that had turned into an unqualified disaster. But she'd never done anything more than kiss. She'd never done *it*. What if she was bad at it? What if she disappointed him? What if he disappointed her?

The pulse at the base of his throat throbbed.

Was he nervous, too?

"Please do not be afraid," he said softly. "I only wanted to kiss you where we do not have to worry about being caught." Then, because apparently her frantic thoughts appeared in a bubble above her head, he added, "I want you to know, I will never do anything you do not want me to do. If you're afraid, or you want stop, all ye have to do is say so."

Her heart squeezed. All her doubts and worries dissolved into the floorboards.

"I don't want to only kiss." With hesitant steps, she closed the distance between them. "I want you to be my first."

His breathing fell into an uneven rhythm, but he didn't reach for her.

Uncertainty nipped at her. "Unless that freaks you out?"

He gave a soft, nearly imperceptible shake of his head. "It doesn't freak me out." With both hands, he cradled her face. "I want to be your first." He stroked her cheeks with the pads of his thumbs. "I want to be the only one to touch you. The first one— the only one—to learn how to please you."

The words tickled a spot low in her belly. He kissed her with slow, drugging kisses that incited a storm of restless arousal inside her. He trailed his fingers down the side of her neck, and then dropped his hands to her waist.

While his mouth continued its delicious exploration of hers, he toyed lightly with the hem of her sweatshirt. When his fingers brushed the bare skin on her stomach, her breath snagged in her throat. Then he tugged the thick sweatshirt over her head, and she stood before him in her skimpy bra.

His hungry gaze devoured her.

A prickling blush spread over her body, and she shivered.

Dark eyes gripped hers, and he held out his hand. Without a beat of hesitation, she slipped her fingers inside his.

At the edge of the bed, he shucked his T-shirt, then helped her lie down on the mattress. He stretched out beside her, and she burrowed close, seeking the warmth from his skin.

His hot mouth tasted the skin on her collarbone and the side of her neck. When his lips hovered above hers, the wild beating of her heart quickened her breath. With shallow, desperate gulps, she gasped at what little wisp of air existed in the miniscule space between them.

"How are ye doing?" He sounded breathless. "You doing all right?"

She couldn't speak, so she moved her head in a curt nod.

He traced the side of her cheek with his fingers. "Are ye sure? Ye seem worried."

"I guess… I'm a little nervous."

His golden eyes shimmered with a warmth so soft and tender she wanted to melt. "About the pain?"

"No, not that." Her cheeks warmed. "I… don't want to disappoint you."

The shadow of a smile touched his lips. "That's not possible."

"I'm not like the other girls you've been with."

A hint of sorrow touched his features. "That's why I'm so certain there's nothing you could do that won't please me."

One callused palm smoothed up her side.

"My boobs aren't big." The confession burst from her as his hand reached the top of her rib cage. "N-not like Sam's, or—or the others."

He peered into her eyes. "There are no others. There never will be another. There's only you." His lips brushed hers. "Always you."

With all of her heart, she wished it were true. She had no idea what the future might hold for them, but most of all, she wished for that.

When he reached for her, his hands trembled.

Her heart wrestled in her throat as he freed first one breast, then the other, from their confining cups. His gaze clamped on her bared flesh as he cupped her in one of his large hands.

Her small breast filled his palm. At the sight and feel of his warm, rough skin on her naked flesh, her lungs constricted. His thumb swept across one pebbled nipple, and a yelp climbed in her throat.

He massaged her with slow, full circles that shot ripples of pleasure to her toes. Swallowing thickly, she closed her eyes.

His hands slid down her body, past her rib cage to the dip of her waist, where the tips of his fingers danced along the waistband of her blue jeans. Slowly, he dragged down the zipper.

The hard thumps of her heartbeat pounded in her ears when his fingers disappeared beneath the fabric of her blue jeans and brushed the crotch of her panties. The yelp escaped her then.

He rubbed over the heart of her, and soon gentle, rolling swirls of delight cascaded from her core and rippled outward. Her stomach muscles clenched, and she moved her hips, chasing the electric shock he delivered to her starved body.

When a greedy moan slipped between her lips, he tugged her blue jeans and panties over her hips and down. She was exposed to him fully when he climbed onto his knees and positioned himself between her legs.

His dark gaze clamped on her face, he reached down, between her legs.

The feathery touch exploded her senses. Desire rushed through her, awakening places inside she never knew existed. With light, teasing strokes, he caressed her everywhere except the spot where she ached the most. She wanted it so badly that she parted her legs, just a little, in hopes that he might want to touch her there, too.

He did.

When the tip of his finger danced along her slit, her head came up off the pillow. The sharp hiss of air she sucked between her teeth morphed into a throaty groan. Her head fell back while his finger probed the entrance of her body with an irresistible gentleness.

He rubbed the sweetly aching flesh in a soft, clever rhythm until she was on fire, her body burning with arousal and the heat of her embarrassment. Helpless to the pleasure, her knees dropped wide.

One finger pushed a fraction inside her, and another moan built in the back of her throat at the delicious promise. He nudged deeper, but then his touch retreated. She whimpered, only to receive the full length of his finger.

A cry tore from her, and she craned her neck to smother the sound in her pillow.

She grew slick, but she was too eager to reach the place he drove her body to be embarrassed. Her breaths came short and ragged while she pleaded with him.

"Yes, *a chroí*. Anything ye want."

Sensation spiraled through her, and she gripped fistfuls of the bedsheets at her sides. Her muscles clenched.

She'd experienced pleasure before, but only by her own hand, and not often since Aiden and his family had moved in. But this, what he was doing to her, was unlike anything she'd felt before.

He lowered his body to the mattress and shifted so his face hovered just above the dark triangle of her curls.

Mortification flooded her, and she reached down to cover herself.

"No, *a rún*." His hot breath feathered over her feverish skin. "Don't hide yourself from me. Please, let me see you."

Hesitantly, she withdrew her shaking hand.

She felt his smile against the tender skin on the inside of her thigh when he quested into her softness with the long glide of his finger once more. He tickled an excruciatingly sensitive spot, and she quivered.

When he pushed a second finger inside her, stretching her body, she experienced a flash of pain that quickly melted into pleasure when his tongue soothed her burning flesh.

Over the quivering swell of her stomach, he peered at her, a gold light in his dark eyes and a slight flush on the crest of his cheeks. A stab of self-consciousness pierced her.

Then, as she watched, he lowered his head and his tongue lashed her throbbing flesh.

Coherent thoughts shattered.

He licked and tasted her, and with every tease of his tongue, swirls of sensation wove through her. She threaded her hands through his thick, soft hair while waves of sensation rushed over her, faster and faster. She worked her hips against the warm strokes of his tongue.

Moans spilled out of her, along with her heart.

He murmured soft demands against her hot flesh, commanding her to open for him and to let it come to her.

Unable to control her shameless reaction to his touches, she pressed her heels into the mattress and arched up into him. Pleasure swelled, then crested.

The shards of sensation splintered through her, breaking apart her soul. Head thrown back, she gripped his shoulders and hung on while the agonizing bliss crashed over her.

She collapsed on the bed, panting.

His fingers still inside her, Aiden kissed and nibbled his way up her body. His hot mouth grazed the sensitive skin near her navel, then the underside of one breast. She had no idea when he'd removed his pants, but his rigid sex brushed against her thigh. His tongue lapped at her beaded nipple before he blew a wisp air over it. All the while, his fingers lightly teased.

"I want to be inside you," he said against the side of her neck.

"I want to please you again. I promise I'll be gentle." His whispers became ragged.

This was it. He was going to make love to her.

A slice of worry slashed at her.

She heard the soft rip of the condom packet, then watched him roll it down his long, hard length.

She swallowed audibly.

Suddenly, she found herself pinned beneath his warm, golden brown gaze. "Are ye sure about this? If ye want to stop, I'll understand."

Her fear dissolved like sugar in a rainstorm.

She didn't understand much about what was happening between them, but she knew that, as long as she lived, she'd never feel afraid when she gazed into his eyes.

"No, Aiden, I don't want to stop. I want to feel you inside me."

His expression crumbled, as though she'd caused him anguish, and he caught her mouth with his.

His lips held hers for a long moment. "Tank you," he murmured against her mouth.

He settled between her thighs, and the head of his sex pressed against her. Reaching between their bodies, he gripped his thick shaft and guided himself to her opening. As he pushed inside, a pained groan escaped him, and his dark lashes fluttered down to lie against his cheeks.

Her slickness eased his passage, and she gasped against the pleasure-pain. Immediately he stilled, his lips parted with his sharp pants.

Beneath him, she wriggled, the impulse to escape his invasion overwhelming. But her movement only drew him deeper.

Fully inside her, a shudder passed through him. "My God, Brynn. You feel so good."

It was the first time she'd ever heard him say her name, and her heart stirred at the sound. The r rolled on his tongue like a purr that licked the growing fire where he'd invaded her.

Stretched and filled, tears prickled behind her eyes.

He dropped a kiss on her temple. "Baby, I'm so sorry. I don't want to hurt you."

Shaking her head, she gripped his wide shoulders, digging her fingers into the solid muscles. "It's not that. I like it, Aiden. I like you."

His golden brown eyes were heavy-lidded when he peered down into her face and, with small increments, began to move his hips.

Soreness dissolved into a fresh wave of need and want. The muscles of his back rippled beneath her fingers as he made a series of short, rhythmic thrusts. Then a groan vibrated in his chest and his rigid length jerked inside her.

Afterward, he remained buried deep, though she felt him soften inside her. She wrapped her arms around his neck, unwilling to let him go so soon after waiting so long to touch him.

He laid his forehead on her shoulder. While his breathing slowed, he lightly stroked the hollow beneath her ear with the tips of his fingers.

It was the most beautiful moment of her life up to that point. Being with Aiden had been nothing like she expected, and so much more than she ever could've dreamed. Sweet, if a little awkward. Sexy, though a bit embarrassing, too.

Nonetheless, he'd made her feel special. Cherished and loved.

Everything about it, about him—about *them*—had been perfect.

Except for the fact that they could never be together.

CHAPTER 12

*T*hat night, she didn't dream. No fantasy could compete with the reality of Aiden lying naked at her side.

In his sleep, the tightness around his mouth softened and the resentment around his eyes faded to a gentle innocence. Her heart light, the sound of his even breathing lulled her into a dreamless slumber.

Heavy darkness cloaked the room when, sometime later, the mattress jiggled. She cracked open her eyes as he climbed from her bed. When he passed by the window, his body momentarily blocked the faint haze of daylight silhouetting the drawn curtains.

She felt his warm presence beside her a moment before he leaned over her and his soft lips brushed her forehead.

The next day, their parents returned home with the baby.

After a hectic day, that night, Brynn retreated to her bedroom and Aiden to his. She lay in bed in the dark, listening to the soft bumps and thuds coming from throughout the house.

When finally all was quiet, his form appeared in the bathroom doorway, which she'd left open in the hopes that he might visit her.

He hovered beneath the archway, and she pushed upright in the bed. Leaning over, she flipped on the lamp and soft light flooded the room.

His expression inscrutable, he remained where he stood on the other side of the room.

Uncertain, she waited.

"I should not be here." The edge of his restraint rode just under his voice.

"I'm glad you are."

Easing back the quilt, she climbed from the bed. As she crossed to him, he gripped the doorframe with one hand and tracked her movements with dark eyes, as though he feared what she might do.

Standing before him, she searched for the source of his hesitation and found it in his serious eyes, where desire warred with shame.

The war broke her heart. She'd never accept that what they'd done was wrong, and she hated that he believed it. Wishing to convince him—and maybe herself, too—she rose on her tiptoes and brushed her mouth over his.

He closed his eyes, but his grip remained latched on the wooden doorjamb.

She slipped her hands beneath the edge of his T-shirt and over the flat plane of his stomach. The tips of her fingers followed the trail of soft hair that ran down the center of his abdomen and disappeared into the waistband of his sleep pants. When she toyed with the drawstring, his eyes flew open.

She slipped the knot and pulled down the elastic waistband. With clumsy hands, she gripped his hard length. Fascinated, she watched her small hand slide down and back up his rigid shaft, his flesh hot and silken against her skin.

After only a few pumps, he was backing her toward the bed and tugging at the hem of her nightshirt as they walked. Yanking the garment over her head, he cast it aside and tumbled with her into the sheets.

His large, warm hands roamed over her sensitive skin, raising a trail of gooseflesh everywhere he touched and rousing a fount of need in her. She parted her thighs, and he nestled between them.

When his hot mouth clamped over one of her nipples, she yelped.

A sound of warning vibrated against her throat. "We must be quiet. They'll hear us."

But another groan slipped from her when his fingers nudged through her springy curls to her hungry core.

Gently, he turned her over on her stomach. From behind, his hand slipped between her thighs, and in one silky glide, his fingers entered her. While he stroked and teased, the callused palm of his other hand smoothed down her back and over the globe of her bottom. Moans built in her throat, and she swiveled her hips, chasing the ripples of sensation his clever touch stirred.

Soon, she heard the rip of the condom packet, then he ran his hand up her back and eased inside her.

Her body opened to him, eager and wanting all he could give her. All of him. Buried deep, he paused a moment before he started to pump his hips. Pleasure built and with every silken slide, her moans grew louder and lustier.

She buried her face in the pillow to conceal the evidence of her climbing arousal. The need to keep quiet somehow intensified the aching desire building inside her, and she lifted her hips to take more of him.

A harsh groan ripped from him and he withdrew from her body. Turning her over, he settled between her thighs and burrowed deep inside her honeyed core once more.

His thrusts grew urgent, needy, and her heart filled with the love he gave. She clawed at his back, wanting to pull him deeper into her body and her heart.

The orgasm crashed over her. He swallowed her cries of pleasure while the luscious waves pitched and plunged her beneath an ocean of erotic pleasure.

With a series of short, hard thrusts, he followed her under.

Every night that week, and the next, he came to her bed. After the house fell quiet and they could be certain everyone slept, he slipped into her bedroom through the adjoining bathroom. They talked some, but mostly he made sweet, carnal love to her, with lots of hushed pleas to be quiet and urgent kisses to silence the lustiest of her moans.

One night, he turned to her, his eyes bright with emotion. "I hate this."

Her heart kicked in her chest. "What do you mean?"

"I hate creeping around." Disgust tainted his tone. "That's the kind of shite me dad used to do."

Tears squeezed the back of her throat. "I'm sorry," she said, because she didn't know what else to say.

"You deserve better."

She bit back the words begging him not to end things between them. "If you want to stop…."

He rolled on top of her and kissed with desperate urgency, so much so that she'd thought he meant it to be their last kiss.

But the next night, he returned to her bed.

Paranoia stalked her as she feared she'd be unable to hide her growing feelings for Aiden from their family. At the dinner table, the temptation was often too much to overcome and she'd sneak a stolen glance at him or forget entirely for a moment that what they were doing was wrong and get lost in her study of his beautiful face.

Then reality would crash into her and she'd shoot a panicked look at her dad, terrified he'd noticed her adoring, lust-filled ogling of her stepbrother.

In truth, no one suspected them. In front of the family and at school, he continued to show her only extreme indifference, and though he halted his wild flirtations with the other girls, on occasion she caught him talking to Samantha Whitaker between classes, only to keep up appearances. Still, he refused even to sneak a stolen glance at her, so closely he guarded their secret.

She didn't mind. Beneath her bedsheets lay their truth.

There, he withheld nothing from her. He didn't banish the tenderness from his eyes or the gentleness from his touch. His smile came quick and easy, and more often than not, she found herself transfixed, both in shock and wonderment of him.

The real Aiden.

He was kind and gentle, lusty and playful, and he gave the best kisses. Not that she had much to compare them to, but somehow she knew no boy would ever kiss her the way Aiden did.

One night, she sat on the bed, rereading passages from *Great Expectations*, which Mr. Strickland threatened would be on their final exam the next day, while Aiden explored her room.

When he slid a book from her shelves, she glanced up. "You won't like that."

Cracking open the spine, he moved toward the bed. "You don't know what I like."

"You read romance novels?"

"Not yet." The mattress dipped beneath him when he settled on the bed and flipped to the first page. "Have you read it?"

She nodded.

"Did you like it?"

Her head bobbed again.

"Can I borrow it?"

She raised the book in her hands. "You're supposed to be reading this."

"Already read it," he murmured, his attention riveted on the text.

Heat crept into her cheeks. "Why do you want to read it?"

His head came up. "I want to know what you like. I want to know everything about you."

The smile remained on her face when she returned to the depressing novel.

"What's this?" he asked a little while later.

She looked over at him.

Between his fingers, he cradled the brass key dangling on a string hooked around her bedpost.

Her gaze dropped to the book. "It's a key."

"What's it to?"

"The front door…" Her throat suddenly dry, she swallowed with difficulty. "Of the old house."

Her heart punched her breastbone with a painful thud, then another, and another, before he spoke. "You kept a key?"

The flash of gold when he flipped the tiny object over drew her gaze. "It was my mom's housekey. I used to think she forgot it when she left, so I held on to it for her." She risked a peek at his face. "In case she came back to get it."

For a moment, he stared at her. Then the key slipped through his fingers. It clattered softly against the headboard while he crawled over to her and claimed her mouth with his.

The kiss wasn't gentle in the way all his other kisses had been. His mouth possessed hers, greedy and demanding.

"You're amazing," he growled as he moved over her.

With rough hands, he shoved the edge of her sleepshirt over her waist and nestled between her thighs. He snatched a condom from the bedside table and rolled it into place. Then, with all the passion and emotion that'd suddenly risen inside him, he fucked her.

He fucked her, and she loved it. She loved everything about it.

She loved him.

She loved his dark eyes and his scarce smile. She loved the way his brown-black hair fell over his forehead while he eased his hard erection inside her. She even loved that his family meant so much to him, despite that very affection being the reason he remained convinced they could never be together.

He fucked her slowly. With his face close to hers, he peered into her eyes.

"You're amazing," he said, repeating his outrageous claim.

As long as he moved inside her, she let herself believe it was true.

He increased their rhythm. Every thrust delivered a surge of desire, pushing out all the love in her heart until she could no longer contain it.

Unbearable pleasure ripped a gasp from her throat. "I love you."

She didn't know what his reaction would be to her confession, but she hadn't expected the smug smile that tipped one corner of his mouth.

"I loved you first," he said.

"You did not."

His hips slowed, and his eyes grew serious. "I did so."

"I loved you, like, the first week we met."

The tips of his fingers brushed the side of her cheek. "And I loved you from the first moment I laid eyes on you."

Stunned, she gaped at him. "You hated me."

"That's what I wanted you to think."

"Why?"

Unable to hold off, his hips inched up and back down. "Because I thought if you thought I hated you, you wouldn't notice how crazy you make me. Hot. Horny. Hopeful."

"Hopeful?" she breathed as his hot flesh pushed inside her.

"That's how it feels to love you." When he kissed her, he tugged gently on her bottom lip. "Like anything and everything is possible."

His love poured from him, and she wrapped her legs around her waist, wanting everything he could give her. After doubting herself for so many years, she relished the feel of his love, luminescent and warm. Soft and true.

With a groan, he dropped his head, pressing his forehead to hers.

Inexplicably, tears welled in her eyes. "I've never felt like this before. I've never felt so... so...."

He found her hand in the dark and, interlacing his fingers with hers, pressed their joined hands to the mattress above their heads. "Me either."

His long, languid thrusts became shorter and less even, and his pleas for her to be quiet were forgotten with his own expanding need.

"One day—" The words clogged in her throat. "We'll find a way to be together, won't we?"

His lips found the side of her throat, and she tilted her head, giving him better access.

The tears that had pooled in the corner of her eyes leaked out. "Please tell me there's a way."

He growled, and his pumping hips drove the doubts and fears from her heart.

When the first voluptuous waves of her orgasm rippled outward from low in her belly, she bit down on his shoulder to stop from crying out his name. His climax sent him hurdling over the cliff behind her.

After his breathing had slowed, he left the bed and disappeared into the dark bathroom. A few moments later, he returned to the bed and slipped beneath the sheets.

He pulled her against him and wrapped his large body around her.

Soon, the rhythm of his breathing told her he slept.

He never did answer her.

But she didn't mind. Not then.

For in that moment, suspended in the twilight of his love, she also believed anything was possible. She had never experienced feelings of such pure joy. Light and warmth.

Hope.

It was a magical moment. A gift of wonder and bliss.

A fleeting rapture, right before it all fell apart.

CHAPTER 13

*T*he terrible roar jerked her from a dreamless sleep.

Beside her, Aiden cursed and stumbled from her bed.

"What in the hell do you think you're doing?" Her dad's booming voice shattered the early morning quiet.

Dressed in only his boxer briefs, Aiden held out his hands at his sides.

Her dad's gaze raked over her, taking in her sleep-rumpled hair and her bare shoulders.

She tugged the covers up to her chin.

"You son of a bitch." The words leaked from between her dad's clenched teeth as a hiss. By slow turns, he faced Aiden. "I welcome you into my home, treat you like my son, and this is how you repay me? By taking advantage of my daughter?"

Brynn clutched the sheets tight around her nakedness and scrambled from the bed. "No, Dad, he didn't—"

Her dad's fist crashed into Aiden's jaw.

She gasped in horror as Aiden stumbled back.

Fury twisted with anguish on her dad's features. "You—you—you raped her."

"Dad, no—" The crack of another fist crashing into Aiden's face wrenched an agonized cry from her.

Aiden collapsed against the wall. He clenched his fists, and the muscles of his chest and torso bunched while he glared up at her dad.

"She's a child." Red splotches mottled her dad's face. "I should call the police. Have you arrested."

"Dad! Stop it, please." She'd never seen him so overcome with rage. Real terror climbed up her spine as he towered over Aiden. "It isn't like that."

When he cocked his elbow, she lunged forward, but her panicked grasps at his arm failed to stop him throwing the next punch, or the next.

Big, meaty fists pummeled Aiden while tears streamed down her cheeks. Screams filled her throat. Why didn't Aiden fight back? He didn't cower, or counterstrike, or even raise his arm to block the blows.

A thunderous roar erupted, and Cian's large body flew by, driving into her dad with a sickening collision of flesh and bone. They hurtled into the dresser, and the lamp perched on top clattered to the floor with a booming bang.

Her dad bellowed in pain. He held out a hand to stay Cian and dragged sharp gulps of air into his lungs.

The baby's piercing cries carried through the house as, slowly, Cian backed away, moving to stand in front of Aiden. Feet planted wide, his eyes blazed and his chest heaved.

Rory slipped into the room and hastened to Cian's side. Together they formed a shield between their older brother and their stepdad.

With a grunt, Aiden climbed to his feet. Blood seeped from the corner of his mouth.

The adrenaline seemed to leave her dad's body all at once. His shoulders slumped and the wild fury drained away, until only the anguish remained.

"You bastard," he rasped.

"Do not call me that," Aiden said in a low, lethal voice.

Her dad hung his head. "How could you do this to me?"

The echo of betrayal reverberated through Brynn. "I love him."

His head snapped up, and repulsion contorted his face. He'd never looked at her that way before. With disgust and bottomless disappointment.

Brynn's heart splintered.

Siobhan appeared in the doorway, jostling the screeching baby, who was bundled tight in her arms.

"You think he loves you?" her dad spat, as though he spoke the most ludicrous combination of words ever to be strung together.

Aiden slipped between his brothers and stepped forward. His dark eyes clamped on Brynn. "I do."

Her dad made a dismissive sound. "The same way you love all the girls, I suppose. You are your dad's son, after all."

"Dad!"

Siobhan gasped and jiggled Brigid more briskly, which continued to have no effect on the baby's wails of protest.

"Brynn, I forbid it."

"I am n-not a child." When Aiden slipped his hand inside hers, she clasped his fingers tight. "I'm eighteen now."

She saw the moment her dad realized that she stated the truth. He expressed no remorse, nor did he offer an apology for forgetting her birthday.

Instead, he set his jaw and stared Aiden down. "This is still my house, and you're no longer welcome in it."

Siobhan gasped her husband's name.

With a tug on her hand, Aiden spun her toward him. "Come with me."

"What?" Her heart pounded in her ears. "Where would we go?"

"Anywhere you want." His fingers brushed her cheek. "Just come with me."

"Brynn Marie, don't you dare even think about it."

At the plaintive devastation in her dad's voice, Brynn turned her head.

Aiden slipped his fingers under her chin and gently drew her face back to his. "We can be together. The way you want."

"What about Samantha Whitaker?" Each word dropped from her dad's tongue like the strike of a sledgehammer.

Each word landed with a gash of devastation on Brynn's heart. She watched the soft tenderness on Aiden's face drain away.

Drawing to his full height, Aiden faced her dad squarely. "What about her?"

"It's your baby she's having."

Pain knifed through Brynn and erupted as a gasp.

"That's not true." Aiden twisted toward her. "It's not true."

"Are you saying you didn't sleep with her?" The hammer of her dad's words thrashed wildly, wringing unbearable agony with each crushing blow.

Dark eyes held her captive, and she searched them, desperate for something that might calm the storm of misery building inside her.

Could it be true? Had Aiden slept with Sam and gotten her pregnant? Brynn tried to recall the exact words he'd told her, but an image of him and Sam talking at his locker only the day before ricocheted around inside her skull and thwarted her efforts to retrieve the memory.

So she peered into his eyes, grasping for something, anything she could latch onto for safety. What she found shattered her heart into a trillion jagged pieces.

Sorrow. Regret. His throat worked.

But he didn't deny it.

"I can explain."

A sob tore from her. "It's true?"

"I didn't say that—"

"What are you saying?" Brynn's dad barked. "That she's lying about being pregnant?"

"I have no idea if she's pregnant or not," Aiden bit out. "If she is, it isn't mine."

"Oh, Aiden." In Siobhan's arms, Brigid squealed her outrage, as though she, too, felt the lashes of sorrow that whipped Brynn.

Aiden seized both Brynn's hands in his. "Brynn, please, come with me." Desperation clawed at his features and abraded his voice.

"Brynn, I'm warning you, if you leave now, I will never speak to you again."

She dragged her gaze away from Aiden. Next to him, her dad appeared slight, even feeble. Grief aged him, drawing deep lines around his eyes and mouth.

In that moment, he reminded her so much of the man he became in those terrible days after her mom left that she blinked several times, hoping the image of her broken, defeated father might change.

It didn't.

Even her dad's deep voice sounded frail. "You wouldn't leave me, would you, pumpkin?"

The way your mother did.

"Brynn, please." Aiden's plea struck her heart.

When she looked at him, his dark eyes glittered with emotion. Unspeakable, unbearable emotion. And she knew whatever words she spoke next would forever seal their fate.

Silent tears falling, she opened her mouth. "I... I... can't go with you."

∾

WITHIN THE HOUR, Aiden was gone from the house.

Gone from her life.

In the days that followed, a veil of misery fell over her. How had everything gone so terribly wrong so quickly?

The horrible scene replayed in her mind on a relentless, torturous loop that left her raw and aching with regret. Had Aiden lied to her about being with those other girls? Had he slept with Samantha Whitaker? Recently enough that she could be pregnant now?

If so, could he have ever really loved Brynn the way he'd claimed?

The barbs of doubt punctured and wounded.

Days turned into weeks, and life went on around her. In sleep, she found no relief from the despair. Awake, she filled her time with distraction, throwing herself into her work at her dad's business for the summer.

But no matter how she tried to block out reality, truth intruded. She couldn't ignore or wish away the fact that Aiden's absence changed them all.

Rory became like a ghost. Rarely was he home, and when he did stay inside the house, he remained barricaded behind his bedroom door.

Cian still appeared at the dinner table once in a while, though he often sported a black eye or a fat lip and always wore a menacing scowl for her dad.

Once, Siobhan asked him about the new bruise darkening his left eye. "What happened to your face this time?"

"Another fight."

"Ye look terrible."

A cruel smile had curled his swollen upper lip. "The other kid looks worse."

Siobhan and her dad no longer flirted at the dinner table or snuggled on the couch. For weeks after that night, neither spoke to the other. Eventually their frostiness thawed, but snuggling was replaced with cool glances, flirting with bickering. They argued about silly, inconsequential things, which Brynn understood was their way of disagreeing about Aiden without ever mentioning his name.

Even little Brigid seemed to feel the loss of her brother. Around the same time every evening, she'd begin to fuss and eventually would work up to a full-blown fit. Her shrill, violent shrieks might echo through the house for hours before she exhausted herself. But despite having worn herself out, she refused to sleep more than a few hours at a time, and Brynn often took turns with Siobhan holding and rocking her through the night.

When school started in the fall, Brynn began her freshman year at Northwestern, where Molly had also enrolled. While Molly made friends and went out on dates, Brynn focused on her studies and worked at her dad's growing company.

One afternoon in mid-October, she popped into a campus café to grab a quick snack between classes, but when she'd paid the cashier for her selection and turned away from the counter, she nearly crashed into Samantha Whitaker.

Brynn reared back. Clutching her sandwich tightly, she gaped at her high school nemesis, who was still gorgeous, tall and slim with large breasts and a flat stomach.

A demonstrably unpregnant stomach.

Over one shoulder, Sam carried a backpack and small purse, but there was no sign of a baby, or a diaper bag, or any of the thousand and one other things Siobhan kept on her person whenever she left the house. Nor did her blouse have any yellowed stains on the shoulders or chest to indicate a baby had recently spit up on her.

A weak sort of half smile twitched at the corner of Sam's mouth before she continued her conversation with another girl in line. She ignored Brynn completely, as though nothing had changed and they were still in high school.

Brynn had no idea what to make of any of it.

That Christmas, Aiden didn't come home.

Nor did he come home for her birthday that spring, as he'd promised her he would.

She tried to forget him, but he persisted in her memory, the way a bright flash of a camera did when she closed her eyes.

The next summer, Brynn packed her belongings into boxes, which she then loaded into the used sedan she'd bought for a few hundred dollars from one of the neighbors. She experienced a small tug of sorrow to be leaving her dad's home, but she was anxious to move into the apartment she and Molly had rented near campus.

Though not nearly as anxious as she was to get away from the memories of Aiden that still haunted her bedroom.

On her way through the bedroom door for the last time, she tossed the old housekey in the trash can. It'd taken her six years, but she'd finally accepted the fact that her mom was never coming back.

She might've worried it'd take her as long to get over Aiden, but she already knew she'd never be completely rid of him. He'd left his mark on her. Her time with him lived like a tattoo on her heart, forever branding her as his.

As another semester slipped away, the tattoo became like a wound that'd never fully healed. It festered and oozed. One day, it might scar or callus over, but all that was dark and gnarly about it would remain inside her.

One day, Aiden would have to come home, and the darkness would be forced out into the light.

One day, though she had no idea when that day might come.

By the time the next Christmas rolled around, she'd developed the torturous habit of wondering what might have been if she'd chosen differently. What might they have become if she'd gone with him? If her dad had never caught them together? If their parents had decided not to get married? If she'd been stronger? If he'd loved her enough to come home? To give her a second chance? If she weren't so riddled with flaws that he didn't wish to at least try?

If... If... If...

If only.

If only the thought of him with another woman didn't bring all the pain rushing back.

If only the threat of the day she'd see his face again didn't leave her feeling shaken and devastated.

If only every time she found the courage to ask Cian or Rory about him, their stilted, cautious answers didn't break her heart all over again.

If only Cian hadn't let slip that Aiden had returned to Chicago for a visit. That he'd been only minutes away and hadn't come to see her.

If only she could get over him, the way he'd obviously done her.

The wound on her heart throbbed with grief and anguish.

He may have loved her first, but it seemed she would love him last.

And while he may wish it weren't so, she knew it wasn't over between them. One day, they'd have to face each other and the consequences of what they'd done.

They'd have to acknowledge what they'd become.

Maybe then, only then, could they ever hope to be free of each other.

The End (of the beginning)

~

Follow Aiden and Brynn as they find their happily ever after in SAINT!

SAINT is the first full-length novel in the Nolan Bastards series and concludes Aiden's and Brynn's story.

ABOUT THE AUTHOR

Amy Olle is the *USA Today* bestselling author of new adult and contemporary romance novels. She enjoys putting her psychology degrees to good use writing emotional, redemptive love stories filled with beautifully flawed characters, cozy settings, and lots of hot sex.

Amy is living happily ever after in Michigan with her college sweetheart, their son, and female turtle named George.

Amy loves hearing from readers! Email her at amy@amy-olle.com or contact her on social media.

Made in the USA
Las Vegas, NV
26 February 2021